PUSHING UP DAISIES

by
Penny Clover Petersen

ISBN-13: 978-1-940758-65-7 Paperback
ISBN-13: 978-1-940758-66-4 E-Pub
ISBN-13: 978-1-940758-67-1 Mobi

Cover design by: Ryan Anderson

Published by:
Intrigue Publishing
11505 Cherry Tree Crossing RD #148
Cheltenham, MD 20623-9998

To my sisters and best friends
Heather, Mary, Chris,
Martha, Lynda Alice, and Linda G.

And to my beloved brother,
Tim Clover

PUSHING UP DAISIES

Holly Hill
September 30, 1814

Dear Mama,

We have been greatly upset by the presence of English troops so near our home. I was prepared to take the children and flee, but Mr. Long, my daring husband, did not feel we were in any great danger.

Since receiving word of our victory at Fort McHenry I breathe somewhat easier, though I wonder what the outcome of this upheaval will be.

I am fortunate that the children are well. Ambrose is fully three and twenty years and a handsome man. It is my hope that our lovely Amelia will soon enter society. I have great expectations for a good marriage. I have set aside the Revere tea set to add to her dowry. The rest of my wedding silver, I think, will make a fine settlement for Matilda and Louise who are flourishing. They are much entertained by Amelia's preparations.

Since I last put pen to paper I have received a most distressing report. Perhaps you would know better how to help my unhappy husband, but I am at a loss. I am ashamed to admit to you that he has been the victim of his own vices and owes a great deal of money in gambling obligations. I find it so difficult to deny him help in this matter, but I fear I must do so now lest he bring ruin to us all.

I spoke to Ambrose only last week and he has promised

that he will care for the girls if I am unable to do so. He has not his father's profligate ways and takes great care of the generous gift you settled on him.

But my apprehension has led me to secrete the girls' dowries on the grounds. I will entrust the location to Ambrose when I see him next. I fear to put the information in writing lest Mr. Long find it and my darling girls lose their chance.

I must leave you for now, dear Mama. I ask you not to worry over much. I have confidence the issue will be resolved in due time. I send you all of my love and hope to visit quite soon.

Your affectionate daughter,
Sophia Amelia Long

> OBITUARY
> Died, at her residence
> Holly Hill in Prince George's
> County, Maryland
> on Saturday evening
> October 1, 1814,
> Sophia Amelia Meade Long,
> aged 42, wife and mother.

Chapter One

"Does howling help?" Daisy Forrest looked at the two little mutts in the passenger seat as she pulled up in front of *The Elms,* the old Victorian home where she and her sister, Rose, shared an apartment over their gift shop. She patted their heads and Malcolm, her own little black dog, nipped her hand. "I guess not." Her mother's dog, Percy, white fur standing on end, continued to wail.

She turned off the car and sat staring into the night while she got a grip on her nerves. Finally, she got out, walked up the path to the porch with Malcom and Percy almost under her feet, and opened the door to the apartment. The dogs scampered in and straight up the stairs. Daisy trudged behind.

She hung her purse on the coat rack in the living room, and took a deep breath. Her sister came in from the kitchen carrying a tray and said, "Oh good. You're just in time to taste this. I call it Spooky Juice. It may need something. I'm not sure." Rose handed her a large martini glass filled with a dark purple mixture.

Daisy grabbed the glass and downed half of it. She threw herself into a chair, decorating her sweater with a good bit of the drink, and gulped what was left. "Do you have any more of this stuff?"

"That good, hmm?" As she refilled Daisy's glass, Rose took a good look at her sister. "Daisy, what's the matter? You look like you've seen a ghost."

Daisy squeezed her eyes shut and grabbed her

short blond curls with both hands.

"Daisy, what in God's name is wrong? Did you have an accident?"

"I saw one."

"You saw an accident? Was someone hurt?"

Daisy opened her eyes. "A ghost."

"A ghost was hurt? What are you talking about?"

"I saw a ghost."

"You did not see a ghost."

"I did too. So did Malcolm and Percy."

"There are no such things as ghosts."

"Yes, there are. And we have just seen one." She took a sip out of her newly filled glass. Her voice sank to a whisper. "It was so weird. We'd dropped Mother off at the airport and I decided to take the back roads home. We were on Laurel Road coming up to Holly Hill Mansion. It looked so beautiful in the distance, glowing in the moonlight. I was thinking how much I liked being a docent there and of how much we still had to do to get ready for our Gothic Evening when a huge ball of fog rolled right across the road. Kind of like a bale of hay, only it was fog."

"Daisy, there's no fog tonight. It's crystal clear outside."

"Well, there was fog on Laurel Road. The dogs started howling when an even bigger bale of the stuff rolled out of the woods. I couldn't see the road. It was freaky. I had to pull over onto the grass. Then the dogs shut up in mid-howl and started climbing onto my head.

"We sat there in this eerie muffled silence until the fog rolled away." Daisy thought a moment. "Well, it might have been muffled because the dogs were covering my ears. Anyway, it was so spooky I just wanted to get out of there. When the fog cleared a little I got the mutts back in their seat, gripped the wheel, and edged the car back onto the road. And there she was. I almost hit her!"

"Hit who?"

"Sophia Amelia Meade Long. She was all wreathed in mist, standing right in front of the car looking at me."

A deep voice asked, "Who?"

Daisy jumped about six inches, completing the sweater decoration. "What the...? Peter, I didn't see you there."

Peter Fleming, Rose's handsome friend, had been sitting quietly in the corner of the room. "Sorry I startled you, but who is this Sophia Amelia whatever?"

"Peter, don't encourage her." Rose got a napkin and mopped up a bit of Spooky Juice from the floor.

"Well, she clearly saw something that frightened her. Why not a ghost? Who is this woman, or I guess I should say, was this woman?"

Rose snapped, "There was no woman. She probably saw a tree."

"I think even Daisy can tell the difference between a woman and a tree."

Daisy pointed at herself and shouted, "Hey! Right here. And I did not see a tree." She puffed out a sigh. "Just what the heck did you mean 'even Daisy'?"

"Sorry. Bad choice of words. I meant, of course Daisy can tell the difference."

Daisy gave him a look. "Hmm, mmm. I'll bet. Well, Sophia Long is the woman who bought Holly Hill Mansion in 1790 and I saw her standing in front of my car not an hour ago. So either it was her ghost or she's looking incredibly good for being two hundred-some years old!"

Rose rolled her eyes. "Okay, let's say you saw someone. Maybe it was a real woman. Sometimes the docents at the Hall dress up, don't they?"

"They do, but it wasn't one of the docents. No one's there at this time of night." Daisy finished her drink.

"What's in this, anyway? I'm feeling a little loopy all of a sudden."

"Well, you're not supposed to drink it like water. It has a bit of this and a lot of that. I thought I'd make a pitcher or two for our Halloween party."

Daisy yawned. "You probably should cut back on the 'that' or everyone will have to spend the night." She put the glass on the table and rubbed her eyes.

"Anyway, there she was, Sophia Long, holding a basket filled with silver. She stared at me a moment and pointed toward the mansion. Then she disappeared into the fog and then the fog disappeared, too."

"Daisy, that's ridiculous. Someone was having fun at your expense. It's almost Halloween. People get creative. Or you saw a tramp or a tree. Anyway, enough about Sophia. And fix your hair. You look like a crazy woman."

Daisy got up and checked herself in the mirror over the fireplace. She patted down her curls and sighed as she looked at the mess on her sweater. "It's not nearly Halloween. It's only October first. And I know a ghost when I almost run into one and this was definitely a ghost."

Peter asked, "How many ghosts have you seen?"

"Well, just this one. But I could tell. She was almost see-through."

Rose ignored this and asked, "Did Mother get off all right?"

"Yes, Mother got off just fine. I think people probably thought she was a very elegant nun. She was dressed head to toe in black."

Rose laughed. "Her idea of appropriate travel attire for attending the funeral of your ex-husband's old auntie."

"Yep. Anyway, she texted me when she got on the

plane. She should be landing in an hour or so. I wish we had known Aunt Lydia better. She always sounded like such a hoot and she was so good to Mother after the divorce." Daisy sat down. "I feel like one of us should have gone with her. I know she needs to say good-bye, but she'll have to put up with Dad."

"Mother can handle Dad," said Rose. "And she was pretty clear about going alone. Where are the mutts?"

Peter pointed to two little tails twitching back and forth under the couch. "Under there. They ran in here like the devil was after them and hid."

Daisy added, "Almost like they saw a ghost."

"Peter, you're not helping." Rose patted his shoulder. "I think it's time for you to go home."

"You're right. It is late. Good night, Daisy. Say hello to your Mrs. Long for me when you see her again." Rose walked out with him.

When she came back Daisy was on the floor saying, "Okay you two. Come out right now. Time for bed." Malcolm and Percy slithered from under the sofa and Daisy picked them up. She carried them down the back staircase and into the garden. Roscoe, their orange tabby cat, was sitting in front of Malcolm's doghouse as if on guard.

Daisy took a minute to admire it. Malcolm's old igloo had been destroyed in a fire not long ago and their neighbor, Ron Tucker, had built him a new house big enough for an entire pack. It was a replica of their own beautiful home. It even had a sign over the door, "*The Little Elms*".

Daisy said, "See, no ghosts here. Roscoe's on duty. Sleep tight." She patted their heads, checked their water bowl, and went back inside.

She entered the kitchen and said, "Well, that drink has knocked me out. Let's clean up and get to bed. We have an early start tomorrow."

Rose said, "Yes, we do."

As Daisy wiped down the counter and put away the vodka and oranges she said, "You know, Rose, it was not a Halloween prank. Nobody would just wait in the woods on the off-chance they could scare the life out of some unsuspecting driver. And where the heck did the fog come from? No. It was not a prank. I saw a ghost!"

The next morning Daisy looked out the bedroom window and sighed. Not a ghost or goblin in sight. Malcolm and Percy were running in the yard. Clearly they weren't letting a little ghostly apparition bother them. Why did it bother her?

Shrugging her shoulders, she looked in the mirror and ran her finger over small lines at the corners of her eyes. "Hmm, not terrible for almost forty." She brushed her hair, then swiped on mascara and blush and was ready for a quick walk before it was time to open the shop.

The Elms was a lovely Victorian home that had been left to the sisters by their great-aunt, Lucille Brodie. The inheritance came a few years ago at a time in their lives when both women were ready for change, so they decided to go into business together. They turned the first floor of the house into a destination gift boutique called Champagne Taste and with a bit of renovating and redecorating of the upper floors created quite a cozy apartment.

So far the arrangement was working. The business had taken off and was making a nice profit. They got along really well and, other than tripping over the occasional dead body, life was pretty good.

Daisy met Rose on the landing above the front door. Rose looked her usual elegant self in a turquoise track suit, her auburn hair pulled into a pony tail. She said,

"What have you been doing? We're late."

"Well, I'm ready now. Let's move it!"

With the dogs on leashes, Daisy and Rose walked up the street toward the bike trail that looped around Old Towne. Daisy said, "I know you don't believe me, but I know I saw Sophia's ghost last night."

Rose shook her head. "All right. Let's suppose that you did see something weird, maybe even ghostly. How do you know it was Sophia?"

"Because she looked exactly like the Gilbert Stuart portrait hanging in the dining room at Holly Hill. You've seen it. She's in a white dress with lace at the bodice holding a fan. Her eyes are a startling deep blue and she has a string of pearls twined in her golden hair. Only last night she wasn't holding a fan, she was holding a basket full of silver. And she seemed to glow. We've always known that she haunts the mansion. A lot of the docents have seen her flitting from room to room. I never imagined she left the house."

"Daisy, someone's playing some sort of joke. Where were you exactly?"

"Just coming up to Dower Cottage. I remember because I noticed that all the lights were on and I thought that was odd."

"Adele's house? Well, maybe you saw her. Maybe she was taking out the trash or something."

Adele Meade Long, a direct descendent of Sophia Long, was the last owner of Holly Hill and now lived in Dower Cottage on the mansion's grounds. She had been a dear friend of the sister's Great Aunt Lucille.

Daisy said, "Rose, it was not Adele and there was no trash. The lights were blotted out by the fog and then Sophia appeared and I freaked out."

Daisy stopped walking and let out a gasp. "Oh my soul, I just realized that when the ghost disappeared, it was totally dark again. The lights in the house had gone out!"

"All that means is that Adele went to bed. So, let's assume that you saw a ghost – which I don't assume for a minute – what's the big deal? I mean, exactly how does this encounter make one bit of difference in your life?"

Daisy stopped walking and looked at her sister. "You're really going to think I'm crazy, but I think she was trying to tell me about something."

"Oh Daisy! You've been watching *Ghost* again. Next you're going to tell me that you and Whoopi Goldberg are planning a séance."

"Rose, don't be an ass. We don't need Whoopi Goldberg for a séance. Although I'll bet that would be a hoot. No, I'm not planning a séance. But the whole thing's just weird. I think I'll go talk to Adele and make sure everything's okay."

Rose said, "That's actually a good idea. In fact, I'll go with you. We haven't been to see her in a while. But right now we'd better move it. I've got a shipment of hand-blown glass Christmas ornaments coming in this morning. I want to be there to make sure that nothing is broken."

Chapter Two

At noon Friday, the shop was empty except for Rose, who was paging through a catalog behind the counter, and one customer casually browsing when their assistant, Tonya Albert, walked in the door.

"Tonya, just in time." She nodded toward the man and whispered, "He can't make up his mind. Wife's birthday. You're so much better at this than I am."

Tonya laughed. "A birthday? That's easy." Walking over to the man who was examining a scarf she said, "Aren't these beautiful. We get them from a small firm in Maine. The wool is sheared from happy little sheep, then hand-dyed and knitted by the most talented artisans. If you're looking for a birthday gift, I think these would be perfect. Does she have a favorite color or, maybe, something to match her eyes?"

Half an hour later the gentleman left with not only a gorgeous azure-blue scarf, but hand-crafted lapis ear rings to go with it.

"Way to go, thanks. I know I've got to get better with customers, but I'd really rather just do the books and inventory."

"Well, I like talking to people. Anything going on today?"

"Not much. Daisy and I are playing hooky. We're running over to visit Adele Long. Will you be all right?"

Tonya had become practically indispensable since she started working for them the previous winter. She was friendly, efficient, and entirely capable of running the shop on her own. An added bonus was that she was dating a local policeman, Tom Willis, so the sisters were able to keep up on whatever happened to be going on in town.

"Oh sure. Anything special you want me to do?"

"No. Things are in good shape." Rose went to the connecting hallway door and yelled up the steps, "Daisy, let's go."

"Five minutes," came a voice from above.

Tonya asked, "Is Miss Long all right? I haven't seen her since last Christmas."

"I'm sure she is, but Daisy's a little worried. Adele's lights were on late the other night. But of course, that was the night Daisy was seeing ghosts, so who knows?"

"She told me about that. I think I'd like to see a ghost."

Rose laughed. "Not you too!"

Tonya looked a little sheepish. "Well, I do wonder. You hear about so many odd happenings, especially at the mansion. Could be ghosts."

"I think Halloween is getting to everybody."

Tonya said, "Maybe, but old houses have long memories and lots of secrets, don't they? And Holly Hill should have its fair share. It must have been hard for Miss Long to give it up."

"Well, I guess you do what you need to. At least when she sold it she knew it would be cared for and not torn down."

"Still, it must have made her sad to leave."

"I know. It was her heritage. But really, keeping it in the family as long as they did was amazing! I mean three of the original dependencies still exist – the Dower House, the kitchen, and the carriage house. That's incredibly rare."

"When did she sell it?"

Rose thought a minute. "Let's see. I think her younger sister, Rosalie, married Fred Walters around 1959 and a year later her parents were killed in a car crash. Aunt Lucille told me Adele was devastated and lonely living in that huge house by herself. Besides, she knew she couldn't keep it up without help. So she set up the Holly Hill Historical Society and sold everything but the cottage to Maryland-National Capital Park and Planning Commission a couple of years later."

"Does her sister live near here?"

"Rosalie and Fred died around 1985 in a car crash like her parents. I remember because Aunt Lucille took us to the funeral. I was just six and it scared me silly."

"Is Adele all alone now?"

"No. She has a nephew, Leo Walters. Not very prepossessing, but nice enough, I guess. He keeps an eye on Adele and seems quite fond of her."

Daisy clattered down the steps and entered the shop through the hall door. "I'm ready to roll."

As they were driving Rose asked, "I've always wondered why Adele's home is called the Dower Cottage? Was there a dowager Meade?"

Daisy replied, "No. Adele just calls it that. It was actually the overseer's house, but that doesn't sound as grand."

"It seems awfully big for an overseer's house."

"Oh, Adele renovated in a big way before she moved in. I've seen pictures of the original and it was just two rooms with a cellar, really. I think they used it for storage."

"How does she support herself?"

"How would I know?"

"You always know everything."

Daisy laughed. "I do, huh?"

Rose said, "I guess I thought working up there you

might have inside information."

"Not a bit. Maybe she lives on the proceeds from the sale. I have no idea."

Daisy turned the car into the mansion's drive, then made a quick left and pulled up in front of a small, white clapboard house.

Adele Meade Long was at her door waiting for them. She was about as tall as Rose, five feet eight inches, but so thin, she looked like a breath of wind would knock her over. Her grey hair was piled on top of her head topped by a dark red chignon, held in place with a mélange of feathers, silk flowers and bobby pins. Her cheeks were dabbed with bright pink rouge, the same color as the caftan she wore, and she had a peacock blue scarf draped around her neck.

Daisy hugged her and said, "Adele, you look wonderful."

"Thank you, dear," she answered in her soft, breathy voice. "I'm so glad you came. Sophia told me she'd seen you."

Rose, who had been admiring the array of plants on the porch, looked up sharply. "Who's Sophia?"

Adele smiled, "Sophia Long, of course. Come in. We'll have a little refreshment."

They sat in the small living room. The coffee table was set for tea with a plate of scones and finger sandwiches.

Adele said, "If you'll excuse me, I'll get the tea. It will just take a moment."

As soon as she left Rose whispered, "Who did you tell about your ghost?"

Daisy said, "Just you, Peter and Tonya."

"Then how does she know you think you saw something?"

"Rose, I don't think I saw something. I *did* see something. And I'm guessing Adele sees her too."

Adele came in carrying a tray with a tea set in the Blue Willow pattern. She poured and handed cups to Daisy and Rose.

Daisy looked at her cup and said, "Adele, these teacups aren't old – I mean, they are reproductions, aren't they?"

"Heavens no. This was Sophia's Minton china. I brought it with me when I moved from the big house. I didn't let Park and Planning have all the treasures." Her eyes twinkled and she laughed softly as she said, "I only use them when I'm entertaining someone who can truly appreciate them. And who is, of course, approved of by Sophia."

Rose, sipping her tea, almost choked. Daisy said, "I know! Be careful with that cup. It's two hundred years old."

Rose shook her head and croaked, "Try the tea. On second thoughts, you're driving. You'd better not. Adele, what kind of tea is this exactly?"

Adele said, "It's a rather nice Scottish Afternoon. Do you like it?"

"You added a little something, didn't you?"

"Well, of course. On a chilly day like this I like a little Jim Beam." She took a sip. "I met James Beauregard Beam, you know, when I was ten years old. He and his wife, Mary, had us to dinner one evening when we were visiting relatives in Kentucky."

"Really? Adele, you should really write things like that down."

"That's what people tell me. Cucumber sandwich?"

Daisy took a sandwich and asked, "Thank you. This is lovely." She hesitated and then asked, "Adele, is everything all right?"

"Yes, dear. Everything is fine. Why do you ask?"

"I was driving by kind of late on Wednesday and I noticed that all the lights were on. I thought you might be sick."

"Oh no. Not at all. Sophia was visiting. Whenever she visits she turns all my lights on. I think she's intrigued with electricity. It must have been very dark at night all those years ago."

"She was here Wednesday night? Does she stop by often?"

"She's a bit sporadic in her appearances. Lately, she's been coming around quite a lot."

"What did you mean when you said that Sophia told you she'd seen Daisy? Does she talk to you?" asked Rose. She had just finished dolloping fig butter onto her scone. She reached out to replace the spoon when it seemed to fly out of her hand and landed face down on the floor.

"Oh, I'm so sorry," she said as she picked it up and gently put it back on the table. "I don't know how that happened."

Adele smiled. "These things do, don't they? No. Sophia doesn't talk to me. But she generally manages to get her message across. I had a vase full of daisies on the table and Thursday morning I found them strewn all over this room. And then when you called and planned a visit – you didn't just pop in as usual – I had a feeling that Sophia was trying to get in touch with you."

"Well I can't imagine why, but she did step out in front of my car Wednesday evening. I almost hit her. She scared me silly. Does she always travel with fog?"

"Fog? Not that I'm aware of. But then I see her here in the house. Come now, let's take a walk in my little garden before you leave. The autumn colors are superb this year."

As they were about to leave Adele's, a car pulled into the driveway. A thin, sandy-haired man in his fifties got out and hugged Adele.

"Leo, you remember Daisy and Rose Forrest, don't you?"

He adjusted his glasses. "Yes, of course I do. How are you?"

Daisy said, "Just fine. How's life treating you?"

"Not bad. I just came by to check on my aunt." Adele snorted. "Aunt Adele, you know I'm uneasy about you being here alone. You are pretty isolated."

"Leo, I'm fine. You worry too much."

"Well, I'm glad Adele has someone looking out for her," said Rose. "Anyway, we have to get back to the shop. It was good to see you."

Rose was quiet on the drive home. As soon as she reached the apartment she logged onto the computer and spent a few minutes tapping keys.

Daisy asked, "What are you doing?"

Rose replied, "Looking something up." She read for a few more minutes and then said, "Holy Minutemen! Do you have any idea what we were using to scoop up the fig butter?"

"I didn't have any. I was freaked out enough trying not to drop my cup. I can't believe Adele uses that china. It must be worth a small fortune. And when you practically threw that spoon on the floor, I decided not to touch another thing. In fact, I'm kind of hungry. Cheese and crackers sound good?"

"In a minute. I didn't drop that spoon. It flew out of my hand by itself. And if I'm right the china was chicken feed compared to the spoon. It had a hallmark on it. A little PR stamped on the back just like this." She pointed to the computer screen. "Daisy, that spoon was made by Paul Revere!"

"Oh, that's impossible. Even Adele isn't nuts enough to use the real thing."

"I'm telling you, Daisy, the spoon had the hallmark

and it certainly looked old enough. Do you think Adele knows what it's worth?"

"If it's real, I'm sure she does. But I don't think the money would matter to her nearly as much as the history." Daisy got up and went to the kitchen. She called out, "You know, maybe Paul Revere visits her too. Maybe he told her we were special and to get out the good silver."

She came back with a tray of smoked Gouda, olives, water crackers, and two crystal flutes with a bottle of sparkling wine tucked under her arm.

Rose asked, "What's with the bubbly? Celebrating Paul Revere's ride?"

"Absolutely. I read an article that said we should enjoy sparkling wines whenever the mood moves us, not just special occasions. So I bought this very nice Prosecco." She gently opened the bottle, poured and handed Rose a glass. "Here's to Adele and ghosts and old spoons."

Chapter Three

At eleven-thirty Saturday morning Rose was sweeping leaves off the front porch as Percy watched when a black Town Car pull up in front of Champagne Taste. A slender woman of a 'certain age' stepped gracefully out. She was dressed elegantly, but completely in black - suit, nylons and shoes - relieved only by the red and blue Boston Red Sox baseball cap she wore perched on top of her ash blond curls. Percy saw her, ran down the walk and launched himself into her arms. Angela Forrest cooed, "Percy, I missed you!"

Rose gave her mother a hug. "Mother, why did you hire a car? We were going to pick you up."

"I know, but I got in earlier than I expected and this was so much easier for you. And the driver was so helpful." She turned and smiled at the middle-aged man pulling two suitcases and a tote out of the trunk.

"Where would you like these?" he said.

"Just leave them on the porch," Rose replied. "I'll take care of them."

Angela took his hand. "Thank you so much."

"It was a pleasure, ma'am. And thank you for the recipe. Sounds good. I'll make it for my World Series party."

They watched the driver pull away from the curb. "Recipe?"

"For a nice little drink I had."

Rose took her mother's arm. "We missed you! Come in. You're just in time for lunch. I think Daisy's got it ready."

They left the luggage on the porch and Angela carried Percy upstairs to the apartment. Malcolm scampered out of the kitchen and flung himself at her. Daisy, right behind, hugged her mother and said, "You're early. Why didn't you call? How was the funeral?"

"I got an earlier flight and didn't want to bother you." She looked a little strained and more tired than usual. "I just needed to get out of there."

"Why was that?" Daisy asked.

"Let's sit down and I'll tell you all about it. Any chance of a cup of tea?"

"Of course. Put your feet up and I'll be right back."

Daisy came back carrying a tray with a pot of tea and three mugs. Angela said, "Oh this is lovely," as she took a sip.

Rose asked, "The funeral was really bad?"

"The funeral was fine. Actually, it was more like a party. After all, Aunt Lydia was ninety-three and was healthy as a horse right up until the end when she got hit by that baseball."

"Leave it to Aunt Lydia to go out in style! But I don't understand, why she was sitting in the cheap seats?"

"Well, you know she absolutely loved the Red Sox and, of course, she had season tickets to Fenway's Pavilion Club. But Monday night when she and her sister, Marie, went to the game, they met an old man with his granddaughter at the gate and traded tickets with him. Marie said they used to trade all the time. They liked sitting in the bleachers on nice nights.

"Anyway, as Marie tells it, it was the bottom of the ninth with two outs and the Sox were down by one with a man on second. Their catcher, Ramon dePietro, was at the plate. He hadn't gotten a decent hit in weeks. Well, to the surprise of everyone, BOOM! He knocks a fastball into right field – only it kept going up into the bleachers and smack into Aunt Lydia's head. Who could ask for a better ending than living well for ninety-three years and then taking one for the team, so to speak? She'd be thrilled to know the Sox won."

"Oh, my lord!" said Daisy. "That poor batter must have felt awful."

"He did, but Marie talked to him the next day and told him Lydia couldn't have gone out on a happier note. She invited him to the funeral. And he came."

"Lydia had already arranged the whole thing, even contacted a caterer and planned a menu. And it was all baseball themed. Now that I think about it, that's rather odd, isn't it? I mean she couldn't have known she'd be hit with a baseball. Could she?"

Daisy glanced at Rose and said, "Maybe she had some inside information."

Angela said, "Hmmm? Well, I guess she could have spoken to someone on the other side. At any rate, it was a real party – hot dogs and peanuts, cold beer, Cracker Jack in big barrels, and we all had these delicious cocktails garnished with pennants that had her name on them. That's the recipe I gave to the driver. You'll like them."

"Well, if it was such a good time, why did you have to get out of there?" Rose asked.

"Too many jack-asses in your father's family."

Daisy said, "Oh. I knew it. We should have gone with you for moral support."

"I didn't really need moral support. I just needed to keep my mouth shut, which I did, but it's always exhausting. I'm glad to be back among friends. What's been going on? Was Percy a good boy?"

Percy, who had snuggled down on Angela's lap, sat up and barked. Angela ruffled his head and said, "So, anything new?"

"Daisy's been seeing ghosts."

"Really? Anyone I knew?"

Daisy laughed and said, "Let's have lunch and I'll tell you all about it."

They had finished eating and were nibbling oatmeal cookies as Daisy finished her tale. Angela said, "Well, that's very interesting. I seem to remember that there's a story about Sophia's silver."

Daisy nodded. "Yes. There are several versions among the docents at the mansion. All we know for fact is that Sophia Amelia Meade was given a silver tea set – teapot, sugar, creamer and twelve spoons –as a wedding gift from her mother. She also received a set of twelve silver tankards, a large bowl and ladle, and a coffee pot. All the silver was made by Paul Revere. They were terribly expensive gifts back then. Today they would be priceless."

"Teaspoons?" Rose asked, "What happened to all of it?"

"We don't know for sure, but I think it's most likely that her husband used it to pay off his gambling debts."

"I thought they were rich."

"*Her* family was rich and, as she was an only child, she eventually inherited everything. Josiah Ambrose Long's family was not, but they were very well connected. He was handsome and charming. He and Sophia were introduced by a mutual acquaintance and Sophia fell head over heels. Her parents weren't crazy about the match, but she had her mind set, so they finally gave their approval. But they did make sure that he couldn't touch her money.

"Sophia and Josiah married in 1790 moved into Holly Hill and filled it with children and a boatload of servants. He began to gamble and Sophia bailed him out. But by the fall of 1814, his debts were considerable and she was afraid they'd have nothing to leave the children. She cut him off. Then Sophia suddenly died of stomach ailment. And a few months later, Josiah died in a riding accident."

Rose said, "A stomach ailment? That sounds a little fishy."

"You're not the only one who thought so. Ambrose, their oldest son, inherited. It was from letters that he exchanged with his sister that we know the silver was missing and that he was suspicious of the way his mother died.

"He thought that his father had murdered her so he could use the silver to pay off his debts. His sister, Amelia, agreed about the murder, but was sure that her mother had hidden the silver from her father before she died so that Amelia would have it for her dowry."

"Old Josiah sounds like a real winner," said Rose.

"I know. It's all so sad. But whether the silver was sold or hidden nobody knows. It's certainly never been found and I can tell you people have looked. In fact, I think someone might still be looking."

Rose asked, "Why would you think that?"

"A couple of things. First, the mansion was broken into last month. Whoever it was set off the alarm, but they had time to get in and move some big pieces of furniture out from the walls before the security company got there. Nothing was taken. Apparently, someone was searching the place. Wally went ballistic."

"And who is Wally?" Angela asked.

"Wally Stone. He's the head honcho. He works for Park and Planning and is in charge of the overall health of Holly Hill. He's not a particularly pleasant kind of guy. He's nit-picky and obnoxious and he does not respect the work the volunteers do. I believe he thinks he owns the house."

Rose frowned. "Okay. I don't understand. Why would someone break in and do that? I mean, it's been two hundred years. No one could think that a silver teapot just happened to drop down behind the sideboard and nobody noticed. What did they think they'd find?"

"Who knows?" Daisy said. "I've heard some idiots believe there are hidden rooms in the house."

Angela's eyes lit up. "Or, perhaps, secret passages – for trysts."

"For nothing at all. There aren't any. But there has been a lot of publicity in the local papers around the anniversary of the battles of Bladensburg and Fort McHenry. I read an article just a couple of months ago about the missing treasure of Holly Hill. People never stop speculating."

"I think it sounds like kids on a treasure hunt." Rose tapped her finger on the table. "What's your other reason? Not that I don't already know."

"If you know, why did you ask?"

Angela said, "Well, *I* don't know. Is there another reason that you think someone is looking for the tea set?"

"Don't laugh. I think Sophia might have been trying to tell me something about the silver when she walked in front of my car."

Angela gasped. "I would never laugh about a thing like that. You could very well be right. Think about it. You said she was holding a basket of silver and pointing to the house. And then that teaspoon flew out of Rose's hand. Yes, I do think she was trying to tell you something."

Rose picked up the last cookie and took a bite. "Why do I have a feeling that you two are going to drag me into some bizarre scheme to either contact a woman who's been dead and gone for two hundred years or go digging for treasure?"

"Honey, I would never drag you anywhere," Angela said. "But I do think we should invite Adele to the séance, don't you?" Rose rolled her eyes and sighed.

The next morning Daisy hurried into the kitchen and grabbed the cup of tea Rose held out to her. "Thanks. I'm going to be late! I'm supposed to be at the mansion in half an hour. Do I look all right?"

"Just like a Holly Hill docent with little black paw prints on your slacks."

Daisy looked down at her ivory pants and shouted, "Malcolm!" She ran back upstairs and was down again in two minutes. She grabbed her cup and the tea sloshed over the top and just missed the grey skirt she had changed into.

Rose said, "Slow down. You're a volunteer. What are they going to do, fire you?"

"Of course not. But sometimes it gets really busy and I hate to leave them shorthanded." She poured her tea into a travel mug, stuck a top on it, grabbed an apple and her purse, and hurried down the hall steps and out the front door.

Rose had just settled into her recliner with the Washington Post when she heard the door open again and someone coming up the stairs.

Rose called out, "What did you forget?" She looked up as Daisy walked slowly into the room, visibly upset.

"What's wrong? Have you seen another ghost?"

"No. Not a ghost." Footsteps sounded behind her and a man appeared in the doorway.

"Rose June, how the hell are you?"

Rose dropped the paper. "Dad?"

Daisy and Rose stood by the mantel forming a united front while Malcolm busied himself sniffing this intruder's pants and grumbling. Dick "Dickie" Forrest stood smiling like a benevolent uncle who just handed over the keys to a new car. He had the looks and charm of Cary Grant, right down to the slightly cleft chin and a hint of an English accent.

"Well, how are you two? You look great. What's with the dog?" Malcolm had apparently decided that the new guy was okay and was gleefully humping his left leg.

Rose picked Malcolm up and murmured, "Not now, you silly mutt." She turned to her father and said, "Dad, what are you doing here? Last we heard from you, you were traipsing around Europe. And that was over five years ago."

"Really? That long? Well, I'm here now. That's what counts."

Daisy said, "Counts for what?"

"Daisy May…"

"Don't call me that. I hate it."

"But it's cute. I named you May after an old aunt. You should be honored. Besides, your mother wanted to call you Fleur de Lis, but I told her, 'This isn't France. Just pick a damned American flower already.'" He sat in Rose's recliner and put his feet up.

Daisy ground her teeth and said, "Where are you staying?"

"I thought I'd just bunk in right here."

Daisy and Rose looked at each other and burst out laughing. Rose finally got herself under control. "Not on your nelly. Why in God's name would we invite you to stay with us? Sorry Dad, but there's a perfect little no-tell motel right down the road. Rents by the hour or the night."

Dick Forrest looked hurt. "I can't believe you would send your own father to a cheap motel."

"Then stay in a pricey one. I don't care. But you're

not staying here."

His face drooped. "I expected a warmer welcome from my girls."

"Really? I can't imagine why. What are you doing here, anyway?"

"Your mother invited me."

Daisy dropped onto the sofa and said, "She did not!"

"Mother invited you here? To stay with us?" Rose asked.

"Well, not exactly. She wasn't specific as to where I should stay."

Daisy said, "Rose, can I talk to you in the kitchen?" Together they left, their father settled in Rose's favorite chair reading the paper.

"Daisy, what was Mother thinking?"

"I don't know, but I'm supposed to be at Holly Hill right now."

"Well, just call and say you can't make it today. You are *not* leaving me alone with him."

"Oh, all right. There's something fishy going on here. I cannot believe Mother asked him to come."

While Daisy called, Rose made a pot of tea and put some cheese and crackers on a plate. Daisy hung up the phone and said, "You're feeding him? He'll never leave."

"I like to think I can be civilized. He is our father. A little tea and out he goes."

They walked into the living room to see Roscoe sitting on the bookcase ready to pounce on the unsuspecting Dick Forrest who happened to be working on the Sunday crossword, Rose's favorite part of the Sunday paper.

Daisy shooed Roscoe off the shelf before he could do any damage and Rose took the crossword out of her father's hands and offered a cup of tea.

"Tea? I rather have something a little stronger, if

you've got it."

Rose said, "We don't. Drink up."

Daisy looked at her father, sitting there as if he owned the place. She asked, "Why are you here, really?" Before he could answer they heard the front door open and the clatter of high heels running up the stairs. Angela Forrest appeared in the doorway radiating fury from every inch of her five and a half feet.

Chapter Four

"Dickie! What in the name of Aunt Fanny Freemantle are you doing here?"

"Angie! You're looking a little pale. Why don't you sit down? I'll get you some tea. I was just telling our girls how you invited me."

"I did no such thing."

"You did. You said, 'You should see the girls.'"

"It was a figure of speech, as anyone with a brain larger than a pea would know. But then you were never the sharpest knife in the chandelier. I was making conversation at a funeral. It certainly was not an invitation. Now go home."

"I don't want to."

Daisy asked, "Mother, how did you know Dad was here? I was just going to call and warn you."

"Yes, Angie, how did you know I was here?"

"I'm psychic. Now I really do think you will be going."

The doorbell rang and Rose said, "For crying out loud, what now?" She ran downstairs to answer it and came back with Peter Fleming just in time to see Angela grab Dickie's ear and pull him out of the chair.

"Ow! Stop that, Angie. Since when can't a father visit his own daughters?"

Angela let go and said, "You always were a whiner." She turned to Peter, "Hello, Peter. How nice to see you again. I'm afraid you've caught us at a rather inopportune moment. It seems we have a rodent infestation."

Rose said, "Peter, this is my father, Dick Forrest. I believe he was just on his way out."

Dickie held out his hand and said, "Actually, I'm in no hurry at all. Always happy to meet a friend of my girl."

Peter shook hands. He looked around the room. Only Dickie was smiling. Daisy, Rose and Angela were not. He said, "Maybe I should come back later."

Angela said, "No dear, you stay. The vermin is going!" and she took her ex-husband by the arm and propelled him out the door. Dickie called out as he was being trundled down the steps, "We'll do dinner tomorrow night."

They heard the front door shut and Daisy said, "Well, that was fun! I could use a little something stronger than tea." She went off to the kitchen and returned a few minutes later with four cocktail glasses on a tray just as Angela came back into the room.

Angela sat down on the couch and Roscoe jumped onto her lap. Daisy handed her a cocktail. She took a sip and said, "Angie! I hate that and he knows it."

"Speaking of names, were you really going to call me Fleur de Lis?"

Angela looked perplexed. "Why would I do that? That would be ridiculous. I had thought about Fleur – certainly no 'de Lis'. I think Fleur is rather pretty. But I was afraid you might get teased."

"Well, thank you for that."

They all sipped cocktails in what was becoming an awkward silence. Finally, Peter said, "This is good. What is it?"

Daisy smiled and said, "I invented it just now. I call it Trouble Named Father." She knocked back the last of her cocktail and said, "Okay, so how did you know Trouble was here?"

Angela said, "Harry called me. He was afraid Dick

was going to do something stupid. Apparently, he seemed very upset after the funeral and told Harry it was time to start mending fences. Maybe he's in a twelve-step program for reprehensible people."

Peter asked, "Who's Harry?"

"Dad's brother."

"The brothers are Dick and Harry?"

"Dick's father was named Tom. He had an odd sense of humor," said Angela.

"I know I shouldn't be asking, but I seem to have walked into the middle of some family drama. Rose, you've never mentioned your father. Why is he reprehensible?"

Rose sipped her drink. "When I was thirteen Dad was supposed to be away on a business trip. However, he was just down the street in a model home. Mother walked in on him as he and their real estate agent were having a rather energetic discussion about sales in the area. After he and Mother had a brief, but passionate exchange of ideas on the subject, he emptied their joint accounts, quit his job with the State Department, moved to Europe, and became an art history lecturer or something. Since then he turns up every six or seven years like a bad penny."

"He left you with nothing?"

Rose laughed, "Well, not so you'd notice."

Angela said, "I have a rather substantial trust fund that Dickie can't touch, so we were not what you could call poor. But he did leave us alone. And it came as a complete surprise to me. I thought our marriage was a good one. But apparently, he wanted a different life. I have never forgiven him, but I like to think I have risen above it. I have to say it's much easier to rise above it when it's in Europe."

"Well, you know he won't be here long," Daisy said. "He never is. Anyway, we've invited Peter and Marc for dinner tomorrow night. You come, too. We can make plans for the séance. That'll cheer you up."

Rose groaned and said, "It's inevitable, I suppose. On the upside, maybe Sophia could scare Dad away!"

Five o'clock Monday evening Rose was taking the pot roast out of the oven. Daisy came into the kitchen and said, "That smells wonderful. I've got the drinks made and the appetizers on the table. What else can I do?"

"Not a thing. I think we're good."

The doorbell rang. Daisy looked at the clock. "I'll bet that's Marc. He likes to come early so he doesn't miss any food."

Marc Proctor was an antiques dealer in Old Towne and Daisy's sometimes date. He was tall, slim, and lots of fun with a boyish charm. Daisy found this boyish charm problematic more often than not. After a short flirtation, a harrowing near-death experience, and the terminal let-down of finding that Marc's moral compass was somewhat skewed, they had decided that just good friends was the way to go.

By five-thirty Marc had been joined by Peter and Angela. Daisy passed the Bees Knees and said, "Sip slowly. They're yummy, but they'll knock you out."

Angela sipped. "Delicious. Well, now that we're all here, I think we should plan the séance."

Marc whose mouth was full of a salami-ham canapé choked out, "The what?"

"Oh sorry. I haven't had a chance to fill you in on my sighting." Daisy proceeded to bring him up to date. Marc shrugged his shoulders and said, "Sounds like a plan," as he ate the last cracker on the cheese plate.

Angela said, "I spoke to Lolita. She's agreed to act as the medium for the séance. She knows about these things."

"Whose Lolita?"

"Lolita Llewelyn is Mother's manicurist," said Rose. "She's also a psychic/palm reader, communer with all animals, and Mother's go-to person for anything not of this world."

"And she's really good at it. This is excellent. Let's have dinner while we plan." Daisy picked up the plates and glasses and started for the kitchen when a voice from the stairway said, "Well, something sure smells great." Dickie Forrest walked in carrying a wine bottle in one hand and flowers in the other.

Rose took the flowers and asked, "Dad? How did you get in here?"

"I came through the connecting door in the shop. You should really keep that locked. Anyone could just wander in."

Angela snorted, "Anyone did."

"Did we have a date?" Daisy asked.

"You don't remember? As Angie was kindly seeing me out yesterday, we all decided on dinner tonight. I was going to take you out, but this is much better. Where are your manners, girls? Introduce me to your friends."

Daisy and Rose looked at Angela. She said, "As I've said, I've risen above. I will not make a scene. He may stay on the condition that he does not call me Angie."

"You always loved Angie."

"No. I did not."

"I think your memory is getting a little fuzzy, but anything to keep the peace - *Angela*."

Rose said, "All right, Dad, you've already met Peter. This is our neighbor, Marc Proctor. Dinner's ready. Let's get this over with."

They had settled back in the living room with coffee and cognac. Dinner had gone as smoothly as possible for an unwanted family reunion.

Dickie had done most of the talking. His fond remembrances of his marriage got so ridiculous that Daisy finally laughed out loud. "Dad, you make it sound like you're getting ready to celebrate an anniversary or something."

Dickie just smiled.

Angela got up and opened the door. "Time for you to go, Dickie. The girls and I have something we need to discuss which has nothing to do with you."

"Not a chance. I want to hear all about this séance of yours. I overheard the story as I was coming up the stairs and it sounds intriguing."

Rose looked at her father. "You were eavesdropping? Really, Dad, aren't you a little old for games?"

"You're never too old for games. So, how do we do this séance thing? You know, I could get in touch with my aunt."

"Dickie, you're not invited. It's as simple as that."

Suddenly the room was filled with Sammy Davis, Jr. belting out, "*I've Gotta Be Me.*" Dickie pulled his cell phone out and said, "Sorry. Have to take this," and moved into the kitchen.

Angela snorted, "I've got be me! That's always been his theme song, all right."

A minute later Dickie came back into the room. "I need to go out for a few minutes. I won't be long. Don't decide anything without me."

Angela waited until she heard the door shut. "Good, now we can make a plan without your father. I don't want him sticking his nose into my séance."

Marc asked, "So, you're going to try to talk to this Sophia?"

"Yes. I think she wants to tell me something," said Daisy. "Okay Mother, what do we need to do?"

"Lolita says we need a group of people with open

minds and, if possible, a relative of the person we want to contact. So I'll talk to Adele. I'm sure she'll be interested. And Rose, you'll have to open your mind a bit."

"I'll do my best."

Marc said, "My mind's pretty empty. Can I sit in?"

"Absolutely." Angela smiled. "How about you, Peter? Care to join us?"

Peter looked at Rose. She nodded. "Sure. I'll be there. Why not?"

"I thought we'll hold it here on Tuesday. There's a full moon. We'll need white roses and a lot of candles. What do you think about incense? Would a spirit like that or not?"

"I'm not sure they can smell," Daisy said. "But incense would add a little atmosphere."

"Incense it is. This is very exciting. Now I just have to figure out what to wear."

By the time Dickie got back everyone had gone and Daisy and Rose were tidying up.

Dickie said, "Where did everybody go? It's early."

"Well, Dad, unlike you, we all have to work tomorrow. So, I guess you'll be off to Europe again."

"No. I'm planning on staying here for a while. I found a little furnished efficiency that I can move into Friday."

Daisy looked at her father. "Dad, just what is going on? Why are you here, really?"

"For the best reason in the world – family. I want to be close to my girls."

"Are you ill?"

"No. Fit as the old proverbial fiddle. I just think it's time to settle down near the people I love. I don't know why no one believes me."

Daisy shook her head and said, "Well, maybe because you haven't seemed to give your family a second thought in quite a while. At any rate, you need to go now. We're tired."

As she was getting ready for bed Daisy stuck her head in Rose's door and said, "What's he up to?"

"I don't know, but I'm willing to bet it's nothing good."

At seven-fifteen the next evening Daisy walked over the oyster shell path to the Carriage House with Sally Henderson. Sally owned a flower shop in Old Towne and was a good friend of both Daisy and Rose. She had recently become a docent at Holly Hill.

Sally stopped for a moment to admire the mansion. "I'm so glad you talked me into volunteering here. This house is so beautiful and the Long family has such a fascinating story."

"It certainly has."

"In fact, working here has gotten me interested in my own family history. I've been doing a lot of research on that ancestry website."

"Anything interesting pop up?"

"Not so far. My family all seem pretty normal and dull. But I have high hopes I'll find some shady characters on my husband's side."

They walked into the Carriage House and sat down. Wally Stone was standing at the front of the room pursing his lips. He looked pointedly at his watch as the other members of the Gothic night committee arrived – Adele Long; Clifton Smith, another docent; Karen Casey, the museum curator; and Marsha Turner, director of the Visitor Center.

When everyone had been seated, he said, "I guess promptness is too much to expect. I should just be happy you made it at all."

Daisy smiled brightly and said, "Well, we're here now."

"First, I'd like to introduce Len Rutherford, my new

second-in-command, to those of you who haven't already met him." A stocky man in his mid-forties sitting next to Wally stood up and saluted.

"He started last month and is still getting the hang of things. I hope you all will help him find his way, if you can find the time, that is."

Adele said, "Oh stop that, Wally! People are busy. They have lives, they work. You should be happy you have volunteers."

Wally sniffed. "Volunteers, yes. Oh well, let's get to the agenda."

For an hour they discussed the status of plans for the upcoming evening - decorations, who would read *The Raven*, docents needed to be on hand, and final decisions about the catering.

At nine Daisy said, "Great. We're right on track. Sorry, guys, I've got to get going. See you next time."

Wally held up his hand and said, "I have one more thing we need to talk about."

Daisy sat back down and everyone looked at him expectantly, but he just sat there staring at them. Then, looking straight at Adele, he said, "I am concerned about the goings-on in this house."

Adele sat up straighter in her chair. "What exactly do you mean, Mr. Stone?"

"I think you know."

"Well, if Adele knows, the rest of us don't," said Daisy. "What the heck are you talking about, Wally?"

"Someone has been in here at night again. Over the past few weeks since the break-in I have found many little things out of order. And this morning I found the door to the butler's pantry open and a custard cup shattered to pieces. It's intolerable. This someone must have a key and know the alarm code. I can only think of one person."

Adele laughed. "Walter Stone, if you think I have

nothing better to do with my nights than traipse up here and break things just to annoy you, you have another think coming. Don't be an idiot, if you can help it."

"Then what is your explanation?"

"It's simple enough. Sophia."

Daisy said, "You could be right, Adele."

Sally Henderson nodded. Karen Casey rolled her eyes and Clifton Smith shook his head. Marsha Turner looked unsure. Wally barked, "That's ridiculous."

Len Rutherford looked puzzled. "Am I missing something? Who is this Sophia? Does she work here?"

"They're talking about our Sophia. Sophia Meade Long."

"But she's dead."

Wally said, "Yes, she is. However, *some* people believe she still lives here which is, as I said, ridiculous. Someone has been getting in here and if it wasn't you, Adele, then I want to know who it is!"

Marsha said, "I have to say I think Wally might be right about someone else breaking in. I really don't think Sophia would break her good china."

Wally looked disgusted "There is no ghost. I think some imbecile is trying to find the Revere silver."

"Have you called the police about this?"

"No. They checked out the original break-in and nothing came of that. What can they do if I can't even find how this person's getting in?"

"Then what are you going to do?" asked Daisy.

"That is my affair. Until I know none of you is responsible, I'm keeping my own counsel."

Daisy said, "Okay. I wish you luck, but it's not easy to catch a ghost."

Wally glared at her and said, "We'll see."

Daisy was almost out the door when Len Rutherford stopped her. "Daisy? You're Dick Forrest's daughter, aren't you? He mentioned that you worked here. You're even prettier than he said you were."

Daisy frowned. "Um, thank you. You know my father?"

"I met him in August at Washington College. He was giving a lecture on Maryland's historic art."

"My father was here in Maryland, in August? Lecturing?"

"Yes. I assumed you'd know that. Anyway, he was a great help. He knew quite a lot about Holly Hill and answered all my questions. He told me you volunteer here."

"Did he? I wonder how he knew that." She smiled. "Well, it was nice meeting you. I hope you come to love this house as much as we do. Good night."

"Daisy, wait a minute. I was hoping we could go out for a drink or something. I don't know a soul here and I'd love to get your ideas about the mansion. Wally can be a bit..."

"Hard to talk to? I know. He does tend to be kind of overly bureaucratic." She pushed the door open.

"About that drink?"

"I'm sorry. I can't this evening, but maybe another time."

It was dark as Daisy walked Adele down the drive to her home. Daisy said, "Did Mother tell you that we are planning a séance? Clearly Sophia was trying to tell me something and that might be the best way to find out what."

"Yes, your mother called me. It's an excellent idea. Sophia has been very active lately, more so than usual. I also suggested to your mother that you might like to hold the séance at the Dower House. Sophia is always near."

"She told me and I think the Dower House would be

the perfect place. But are you sure? You'll have a houseful."

"Yes, dear. I'm sure."

They were nearly at Adele's door when they saw what looked like a little flame, maybe from a candle, moving through the trees to the left of the path.

Daisy whispered, "What is that?"

"It seems to be a candle floating in the air." Suddenly a bale of fog rolled across the path and into the trees. They heard a grunt and the flame went out.

Daisy gasped. "I just can't get used to that fog."

"My goodness. I see what you mean."

They waited for Sophia to appear, but nothing more happened. Daisy walked Adele to her door and said, "Will you be all right?"

"Of course, dear. Why wouldn't I? Sophia and I are old friends. Good night. I look forward to our meeting next Tuesday."

Chapter Five

"Did you know Dad was here in August?" Daisy asked later that evening as she made herself a cup of tea and grabbed a cookie from the jar.

"Here?"

"In Chestertown."

"No. How do you know?"

"Len Rutherford told me."

"Who's that?"

"Wally's new assistant. I just met him tonight and he mentioned that Dad had told him about my working at Holly Hill."

"That's odd. I realize Dad isn't the most enthusiastic parent in the world, but you'd think he'd at least drop by when he's in the area."

"I know. And it's also odd that Dad seemed to know a lot about Holly Hill, including the fact that I volunteer there. I'm sure he's up to something, but I can't figure out what it could be."

Later as Rose was brushing her teeth Daisy popped her head in and said, "I almost forgot to tell you. Sophia dropped by Adele's again this evening. Only this time it was just a candle bobbing around in the trees. Then the fog came and put it out."

"Maybe she's melting."

"That's witches."

"Go to sleep."

The next night Rose was closing out the register

when Dickie Forrest walked in and slapped a large box down on the counter. "I come bearing gifts. Look at this! I got us a Ouija board. I thought the three of us could ask it some questions. What do you think?"

"I think the whole family is going nuts."

Daisy walked in from the sunroom and said, "What are you doing here?"

"Daisy, I thought you might like to get in touch with the other side." Daisy looked at the box on the counter and said, "Ooh! A Ouija board."

Dickie grinned and said, "I thought you'd like it."

"This does not change a thing, you know. But I've always wanted to try the Ouija."

"Great!" He started to open the box. "What do you want to know?"

Daisy shook her head. "No. We have to do this right. We'll close up first and have some dinner. We'll think about who to contact."

Rose looked at the two of them grinning happily and sighed. "Pepperoni for three?"

The sun was setting as Daisy lit candles and placed them around the sunroom and her father set the Ouija board on the little table and moved three chairs to one side of it. Rose, standing in the doorway watching them, sipped a Séance Surprise, a little something concocted by Dickie just for this occasion.

She said, "You may leave a lot to be desired as a parent and I'm beginning to believe that you have a few screws loose, Dad, but I have to say that you make a pretty good cocktail."

"I do, don't I. Years of practice. And I thought we should be well oiled for this little trip to the unknown."

Rose asked, "So, what do we do?"

Daisy clapped her hands. "Sit, sit, sit." They all sat. "I looked it up on-line - how to talk to the Ouija. You can find anything on YouTube. It's great. First, it said we need to clear our minds. And we need to come to the table with only good intentions. They recommend meditating for a minute." She took a deep breath and closed her eyes. Dickie did the same. Rose just sipped and waited.

Daisy opened her eyes and said, "Now, we place two fingers on the planchette and chant."

Rose looked puzzled. "What's the planchette?"

"The pointer! Now quiet. We all need to chant."

"What?"

"What do you mean - what? We chant."

"Yes. But what do we chant?'

"Oh. We say, 'Ouija, are you there?'"

With fingers properly in place, they chanted. Suddenly the pointer slid across the board to the *Yes* in the corner.

Daisy drew in a breath. "It's working! All right, Dad. This is your board. Who do you want to talk to?"

Dickie smiled and said, "I think I need to try Aunt Lydia. She should be easiest to contact since she's only been gone a couple of weeks, don't you think?"

"Okay. Aunt Lydia. Now you're supposed to call her name and ask if she's here," said Daisy.

Dickie took his time. He closed his eyes again and intoned, "Lydia Forrest, are you here?"

The pointer began to move. I A M. Daisy whispered, "She's here!"

Rose snorted. "You're moving it."

"I am not."

"Then Dad is."

"Not I."

Daisy said, "Quiet. Aunt Lydia, this is Daisy. I just wanted you to know the Red Sox won that game."

"Daisy, that's ridiculous."

"Why? She loved the Sox. I'll bet that would make

her day."

Dickie held up his hand. "Girls, let's not be silly." He replaced his fingers. "Lydia, we're concerned. Are you happy?"

The pointer moved again. N O

"Oh, that's terrible," Daisy said. "Ask her how we can help."

Dickie spoke slowly. "Lydia, what can we can do to make you happy?"

The pointer kept moving deliberately over the letters. Daisy said, "Oh wow. She's writing something. R D, no E, C O N C J, no I…"

Malcolm, who'd been lying under the table, yipped, just as *'I've Gotta Be Me'* rang out and totally broke the mood. The pointer stopped moving.

Dickie looked at his phone and said, "I'll take this in the shop."

"Shoot," said Daisy. "We should have written that down. Do you remember what the letters were?"

Rose held up a sheet of paper. "Actually, I did write it down."

"You do believe! Hah."

"No. I don't think Aunt Lydia was here. I just wanted to see what Dad was spelling. He's trying to get in our heads with something."

Dickie came back in and said, "Sorry girls, I hate to leave in mid-message, but I've got to go. Bye Lydia, wherever you are. We'll finish this another time."

Later, as Daisy sat in her favorite chair with Roscoe on her lap reading and re-reading the message she said, "Well, it's too bad she got cut off. I can't figure out what Lydia was trying to say."

"She wasn't. It was Dad."

"Then he's doing a lousy job. This doesn't spell anything."

Pushing Up Daisies

Holly Hill was open for tours on Friday and Sunday afternoons. Daisy normally worked Sundays, but a book group had requested that she give them a special tour that Friday.

She got to the mansion at one and stopped in the Visitor Center. Marsha Turner and two of the other docents, Joy Phillips and Alice Joseph, were already there working in the gift shop.

Marsha said, "I didn't know you were in today."

"It's a special tour for some book group. Do you know anything about them? They asked for me and I can't imagine why."

"Let me check." Marsha pulled up the calendar on her computer and said, "Here it is. Highview Book Club. No contact person. Maybe one of them has been here before and liked the tour you gave."

Daisy shrugged. "Could be, I guess. Anyway, they should be here in half an hour. Is the house unlocked?"

Marsha shook her head. "I was just getting ready to go over and open up."

"I'll do it. I think I'll just make sure our late night visitor hasn't struck again before the readers get here. You can send them over as soon as they arrive."

Marsha said, "All right. Thanks," and handed Daisy the keys.

Daisy walked across the oyster shell path, unlocked the east entrance door, and turned off the alarm. Walking along the hall that ran the entire width of the house, she made her way to the servants' staircase in the west wing and up to the second floor. She went through each of the bedchambers, then took the main staircase in the center of the house down to the first floor and walked through the parlor, dining room, office and butler's pantry. Everything seemed in order.

Daisy checked her watch and decided she had just enough time to take a quick look at the basement.

The basement consisted of four rooms with an uneven brick floor and stone walls. The staircase opened into a large room running the width of the house on the north side. The only door to the outside was set in the center of the north wall and led to the buttery under the front portico of the house. It was padlocked and never used. On the south side were the old servants' hall on the east end and a wine cellar on the west end. A storage area sat between the two rooms behind wooden lattice doors set into two low stone archways. It was chilly and dim, only a little daylight coming in from the small casement windows set high in the north wall.

As Daisy stepped off the staircase a shiver ran up her spine. She called out, "Anybody here? Sophia, are you haunting today?"

Daisy switched on a wall lamp. She looked into the usually empty servants' room to see a new display of 19th century clothes on one side of the fireplace and on the other side a portable bulletin board with a copy of the original deed to the property and an intricate Long family tree posted on it. A small table containing kitchen tools had been added and the fireplace was decorated with a Dutch oven, andirons, and a heavy black kettle.

She passed the storage area and noticed that the door was ajar. As she was fastening the latch she thought she saw something through the lattice on the rear wall. "What is that?" she wondered.

She ducked under the arch and was reaching for the overhead light when a gust of wind blew across the room. She turned around, stumbled on a loose brick, and fell against the arch. "Get hold of yourself. Even if she's hanging around, Sophia is a friendly ghost." She laughed and ducked her head as she hurried out of the storage area. "Okay, now I'm having whole conversations with myself."

Clouds scudded across the sky limiting what little light there was and the gloom descended on Daisy like a blanket. She flicked the switch on the light fixture on the west wall, but the bulb must have been dead. She stepped into the wine cellar. Everything seemed to be where it should be - a couple of wine barrels on the south side, a bottling table, and the hundreds of bottles resting in their alcoves. She breathed a sigh of relief. "All good. I'm out of here." But as she turned to go she realized that she had stepped in something sticky.

"Yuk! What is that?" She pulled her phone out of her pocket and shone the flashlight on a puddle of dark goo under her shoe. She followed the little trail across the bricks with the beam to the south wall. She gulped as she looked at a foot sticking out from behind the largest cask and whispered, "For crying out loud, not again!" She edged her way around the puddle and stared at the body behind the keg. Wally Stone's dead eyes stared right back. He was lying on the bricks, a little smirk on his pursed lips and a large crack in his bald head.

For several moments Daisy just stood there looking at poor old Wally. Finally, she reached down and touched his throat looking for a pulse she knew was not there.

She was backing out of the room and had just started to dial 911 when she heard footsteps at the top of the stairs. She thought, "Oh, lord, they're here." She called out, "Just a minute," and moved to head off any inquisitive booklovers.

Whatever she had stepped in, and she really didn't want to think about what it was, made her shoes so sticky that she left them in the doorway and quickly mounted the staircase. When she got to the top she almost fainted. Sophia Long was standing there in her white gown with lace at the bodice and string of pearls twined in her hair.

"Surprise!" Angela Forrest beamed as she twirled around.

Daisy shrieked, "Oh my God. Mother? What are you doing here?"

"It's my book club. I wanted to surprise you. The rest of the ladies are on their way."

"You scared me half to death. Why are you dressed like that?"

"We thought it would be great fun if we all dressed like Sophia today. I'm the elegant evening Sophia. The others are coming in a nightdress, a day dress, and Sunday go-to-meeting clothes. I thought you'd love it."

Daisy sighed. "Normally, I would. But not today. We can't have a tour today."

"What's wrong?"

"Wally Stone's in the basement."

"And he's being officious again?"

"Nope. He's just being dead."

Chapter Six

An hour later, Daisy was sitting on the bottom step of the grand staircase in her blue wool sheath and wearing a pair of acid green garden boots covered with lady bugs. Rose sat beside her. Police and technicians were moving around the house.

"What is it with us?" Rose said. "Do you think we have a dead body magnet or something? I mean this is third in less than two years!"

Daisy held her head in hands and said, "I don't know. Why are you here, anyway?"

"Mother called. She said you needed shoes. And I figured you could use the moral support. Sorry. The boots were the first things I could find. They kind of ruin the line of that beautiful dress."

"They're fine. Thanks – for the footwear and the support. I stepped in something when I found him. I'm afraid to think what." She sighed, "Wally wasn't the nicest man, but..."

"I know. Has anyone talked to you yet?"

"Some patrolman took a statement and told me to wait here."

She got up, walked to the window and stared at the row of chrysanthemums lining the drive. "This doesn't seem real. I am totally freaked out. Mother scared me half to death dressed like that. And then Len Rutherford turned up being way too sympathetic. I think he wanted to stay with me and hold my hand until I convinced him that he should probably be watching what the police were doing to the house."

"I haven't met him, yet. What's he like?"

"A little oily, to be honest. But when he got going he seemed to be stepping right into Wally's shoes. He ran around behind the police practically sobbing whenever they touched something. Where did they stash Mother and the book club?"

"Mother went down to Adele's to let her know what's going on and make sure she's all right. The other ladies are in the Visitor Center. Did you see them? They're all wearing blond wigs. Dot's wearing a mob cap, bloomers, stockings, a chemise, and a corset topped off with a red velvet cape. She sort of looks like Queen Latifah as a Colonial super-heroine gone berserk."

Daisy laughed. "That she does. I had to head them off before they came in here. They certainly made an odd little parade walking cross the oyster shells."

"Ms. Forrest?"

Daisy jumped at the sound and turned to see Josh Lucas, her favorite actor, standing there looking just as charming as he did in the movies with his piercing blue eyes and just the hint of a southern drawl.

She stammered something unintelligible, then blushed right up to her ears.

"Ms. Forrest?" he asked again.

Rose poked Daisy's arm.

Daisy mumbled, "Huh?" and continued staring open-mouthed.

Rose pointed at Daisy and said, "She is Ms. Forrest."

"And you are?"

Rose answered, "Well, actually, I'm Ms. Forrest, too. I'm Rose, but I'm just an innocent bystander. This is my sister Daisy, the one who found the body. Apparently, I'm going to be her interpreter." She shook Daisy's arm and whispered, "Get a grip, you idiot."

Daisy shook herself. "What? Oh, I am so sorry. I thought I was someone else."

"I see. Ms. Forrest. I'm Detective Brian Hathaway, Prince George's County Homicide."

"Of course you are. Who else would you be? I'm Daisy Forrest. This is my sister, Rose."

Rose poked her again. "We did that already."

Daisy said, "We did? Good to know."

"Ms. Forrest..."

"Call me Daisy."

"Ms. Forrest, I need to ask you a few questions."

"Sure. Ask away."

Rose said, "Does she need a lawyer?"

Daisy squinted at her sister. "Why would I need a lawyer?"

"I don't know. To be on the safe side."

"The safe side of what? I just found the poor schmuck."

Detective Hathaway looked a little bewildered. "Um, if you'd like a lawyer you can call one. But really I just need to know how you came to find Mr. Stone."

"I don't need a lawyer, but I sure could use a little something." She looked thoughtful. "What do you think about a gimlet? That's the one with gin and lime juice, right?" Rose nodded. "I think that would really hit the spot right now."

"Ms. Forrest!"

"I'm sorry Detective, but finding dead bodies always makes me thirsty."

"Always? Do you find a lot of them?"

"More than you'd think. I mean some people go through their entire lives without so much as tripping over a dead mouse, but Rose and I seem to attract them. Bodies, I mean, not mice."

He rubbed his forehead and said, "Ms. Forrest..."

"Daisy."

"Okay. Daisy. Can you tell me what happened here today?"

"Oh, right. Well, I found poor Wally Stone dead as a doornail." And Daisy told him how she came to find the body.

"Do you have any idea what he would be doing in the wine cellar?"

"You know, I think I do. He was either trying to catch an intruder or, possibly, Sophia Long. There are varying opinions about who has been getting in."

"Come again?"

Daisy told him about the furniture, the broken china, and Wally's secret plan to catch the culprit. "How was he killed? Do you have the murder weapon? Was he moved?"

"Ms. Forrest." At a look from Daisy, he said, "Sorry, Daisy. I'm just beginning this investigation. If there's anything you should know, I'll be sure to tell you. We'll need a written statement. Can you come by the station tomorrow morning?"

"Of course. Will you be there?"

"I'm not sure. But there will be someone to take it all down."

Just then, Angela came in through the front door her wig tilted to one side. The pearls that had been entwined were now sticking out like little spikes. And a smear of fingerprint dust ran down the front of her dress. Hathaway stared at her as she adjusted her wig and wiped at the smudges. "That dust seems to be everywhere."

"Well, ma'am, you really aren't supposed to be in here."

Daisy said, "Detective Hathaway, this is my mother, Angela Forrest. She belongs to the book club I was going to give a tour to."

Angela smiled. "So pleased to meet you. Of course,

I wish the circumstances were more pleasant. And I certainly don't mean to get in the way. I know you have quite a job to do here, but I had a thought. The girls and I are holding a séance on Tuesday and I will be happy to ask Sophia if she knows who did this. She might give you a good lead."

Rose held up her hand. "Mother, I really don't think Detective Hathaway wants to hear about séances. Do you, Detective?"

He shook his head. "Not really. I think I've got enough for the moment. You ladies may as well go home and have your gimlets."

Angela clapped her hands, "Gimlets! Perfect. Why don't you drop by? We have drinkie-poos at six. We'll raise a glass to poor Wally Stone."

By six-thirty Daisy was on her second cocktail. She was sitting on the patio wearing a paint-stained sweatshirt, baggy black sweatpants, and sock-monkey slippers. Roscoe was curled up on her lap. Rose was at the grill cooking chicken and Angela was playing with the dogs.

Daisy asked, "How was Adele? I'm kind of worried about her."

"She was fine. Leo was with her when I got there. He said he'd stay the night, but Adele told him he certainly would not. I quite understand that. Nobody her age wants to be looked after. And I'm sure Sophia will keep her safe."

"More likely her alarm system will. And the police," said Rose.

"Speaking of police, I thought Detective Hathaway was rather attractive." Angela gave each dog a treat and shooed them off.

Rose laughed. "Well, Daisy certainly thought so. You should have seen her, Mother. She couldn't get a word out. And then when she did, she just babbled on like a crazy woman."

"I did, didn't I? Oh God, he must think I am a crazy woman. But he startled me. He had no business sneaking up like that and looking like Josh Lucas."

"And we all know how you feel about him."

Daisy glared at her sister. "It was incredibly embarrassing. There I was standing in those stupid green ladybug boots. When I got home I realized that something had gotten on the front of my dress, sort of strategically placed if you know what I mean. I looked like I had two little grey targets pasted on my chest." She shook her head, "With any luck I'll never have to see the man again. I'll just give my statement to some lackey tomorrow and that's all she wrote."

"Perhaps you're being a little premature." Angela looked past Daisy and said, "Well, look who's here."

Detective Brian Hathaway stood at the gate holding a pair of shoes in a plastic evidence bag. "I hope I'm not interrupting."

Daisy shrieked, "Shoot!" She jumped up unceremoniously dumping Roscoe on the floor and ran inside.

Rose opened the gate and said, "Come in. You're not interrupting a thing. Can I get you a drink? Or are you on duty?"

"Actually, I'm off duty and a drink would be great. It's been a long day." He looked at the back door. "But I do need to talk to Daisy."

Angela said, "She'll be right back. She probably heard the phone."

A few minutes later Daisy came out again, casually elegant in strappy sandals, skinny jeans and a blue sweater that matched her eyes, carrying a bowl of cat food. "Detective Hathaway, what a surprise. I was just feeding the cat." She put the bowl down and called to

Roscoe who gave her a condescending look and walked away.

Brian Hathaway handed the evidence bag to Daisy. "I figured you might need your shoes. The boots looked cute, but I'm guessing they don't really go with the dress."

She took the bag, holding it at arm's length. "I'm not sure I want them. Was I standing in, you know, bodily fluid?"

"No. It seemed to be some sort of drink, maybe a smoothie. We're not sure what was in it and we're still trying to figure out how it got there."

"Oh, thank God. I don't think I could have worn them again if I'd been wading around in Wally juice. But you really didn't have to bring my shoes back yourself. I could have picked them up."

"It was no trouble. And I needed to ask you about this Sophia woman."

"Sophia?"

"Yes. You mentioned someone named Sophia a couple of times, but I didn't follow up. Who is she and where can I find her?"

Rose burst out laughing and handed him a glass. "You're going to need this."

Angela said, "It's no laughing matter, Rose. Sophia probably knows exactly who killed Wally Stone!"

"Well, Detective, Sophia is a little hard to find," said Daisy. "She, sort of, shows up when she wants to. And I'm not sure she'll talk to you."

Brian Hathaway looked serious. "I'm sorry, but that's not the way it works. I'll get a warrant if I need to."

"You don't need to do that. I'm sure she'd like to help. It's just very hard communicating with her. But as my mother mentioned, we are having a séance on Tuesday and I think we'll be able to get in touch with her then."

Detective Hathaway took a large swallow of his drink. He looked at the three women, at Percy sleeping under the tree, at the cat curled up in the flower bed and at Malcolm sniffing his shoe. "You all look pretty normal."

Rose filled his glass again and said, "I told you. They believe in ghosts. Sophia is Sophia Long, the woman who built Holly Hill all those many years ago. Daisy thinks she's seen her. I think she's nuts."

"I *have* seen her. And she was trying to tell me something."

Rose was taking the chicken off the grill. Brian Hathaway noticed and said, "Okay then. I can see that dinner's ready, so I'll get out of your hair." He gave Daisy a long look. "Be sure to let me know if this Sophia tells you anything."

He dislodged Malcolm who was now attached to his leg and stood up. Angela said, "Oh, stay for dinner. At least have some guacamole."

Daisy said, "I know this all sounds ridiculous, but it isn't really. And I would like to thank you for bringing my shoes by. We've got plenty of food and not a specter in sight."

Brian Hathaway laughed and said, "All right. That chicken smells good and I haven't eaten since this morning. But I have to warn you, I'm not a big believer in ghosts."

Chapter Seven

"I think he likes you. Why else would any sane person sit there and listen to you and Mother go on about ghosts? And he did bring your shoes by when he really didn't have to. He could have just called you and asked about Sophia."

Daisy and Rose were doing the last of the kitchen clean-up. "I don't know about liking me. Apparently, he tried to call me on my cell, but it just went to voicemail."

"Maybe the battery's dead."

"I just charged it." Daisy reached into her pocket, but the phone wasn't there. "Where did I put it?"

She checked her purse, the desk, her dresser. Rose picked up the landline and dialed, "I'm calling you. Go find yourself."

Daisy walked all over the apartment. "It's not here."

"Check the car."

She ran out to the car, nothing. She walked back in and said, "I must have left it at Holly Hill."

Rose said, "Of course! Well, you can get it next week."

"I can't wait a week." She thought a minute. "I've still got the key. I can run over there tomorrow after we close and pick it up."

"I'll go with you and we can go for pizza afterward."

"All right." Daisy sighed. "How sad is that? My sister is my Saturday night date."

Daisy yawned as she hung her blue dress on the

back of the closet door to remind her to take it to the dry cleaners, changed into her nightshirt and hopped into bed. She picked up the latest Alan Bradley from her night table and began to read. An hour later she jerked her head up and caught the book as it was sliding out of her hands. She put it on the nightstand, turned the lamp out, and screamed.

The next thing she knew the overhead light came on and Rose was standing in the doorway with a baseball bat. "What's wrong?"

Daisy looked across the room. "Turn off the light."

Rose flipped the switch and gasped. The two spots on Daisy's dress were glowing like weird luminescent eyes. "What is that?"

"I don't know. I thought it was just some sort of dust or something. But I've never heard of dust glowing in the dark."

Rose examined the spots. "How did you get it on there?"

"I have no idea." Daisy thought a minute. "It must have been at the mansion. That's the only place I've worn it."

"It feels sort of like paint. Have they been doing any work up there?"

Daisy thought for a minute. "I don't think so. And I didn't touch anything, anyway!"

"Well something touched you. I'm afraid this might not come out, whatever it is." Rose yawned. "Oh, let's go to sleep. We'll figure it out tomorrow."

It was nearly dark when Daisy pulled up in front of Holly Hill the next evening. She turned to Rose, "I'll just run in and get the phone. I think I know where I must have left it."

"You want me to come with you?"

"No. I can handle this. I'll just be a minute."

Daisy got out and headed toward the side of the house. It was quiet as she tiptoed her way along the path. The sun sank leaving Daisy standing in the darkness. She shook herself and said, "Get a grip, you idiot." As she reached for her key the motion sensor light sprang on. Daisy jumped about a foot and ran back to the car. "Okay, Rose, you can come with me."

"I thought you might want company."

They got to the door and Rose said, "Daisy, the police tapes still up. We can't go in."

"What's a little tape among friends? I need my phone. I was going crazy without it all day."

"You should have called Brian. He could have gotten it for you."

Daisy put the key in the lock and started carefully pulling the tape away. "Well, I didn't. It's not like we're breaking and entering. I have the key and the alarm code."

She eased the door open. The green light on the alarm panel was glowing and she quickly entered the code.

"Where's the light switch?" asked Rose.

"I don't think we should turn it on. Technically, we're not supposed to be here."

Rose snorted. "Technically? What happened to, 'I have the key and the alarm code'?"

"Well, I do have the key. I just don't want to advertise that we're here. I brought a little flashlight." She shone the weak beam down the hall and they moved toward the main staircase. Daisy said, "I must have put it down around here." She was shining the little light all over the area and Rose was feeling all the surfaces.

"I can't find it. Where else were you? Retrace your steps."

Daisy said, "I looked around upstairs, then went to the cellar. I know had it when I was down there."

"Okay. Let's do it, just like you did yesterday."

Daisy looked uneasy. "I don't know."

"Well, I do. You're not going to relax until you find the dumb thing, so let's find it."

Daisy led the way down the steps into the basement. "Careful, these stairs are tricky." She stopped at the bottom and Rose almost ran into her. Rose said, "Turn on a light or we'll kill ourselves."

Daisy switched on the wall light.

Rose asked, "All right. What did you do when you got down here?"

"I looked into the servants' room and then I walked over to the wine cellar." She stopped moving and said, "No, I didn't. I went into the store room when I noticed something on that back wall. I was reaching for the overhead light chain, so I could see what it was, but Sophia decided to blow on my neck and I got scared. Then I stumbled into the archway in my hurry to get out."

They walked into the storage room and Daisy pulled on the light. Rose looked around. "I don't see anything."

Daisy turned the light off for a moment. Rose said, "I still don't see anything. What did it look like?"

"Sort of glowy, like the stuff on my dress. In fact, thinking about it I must have gotten it on me in here when I stumbled." She turned the light on again and examined the archway, but saw nothing but old white paint. She turned around and faced the rear wall. "I know I saw something right back there."

"Well, it's not there now." Rose rubbed her sister's shoulder. "Let's find the phone and get out of here. What did you do next?"

"I looked in the wine cellar and almost missed him. If it weren't for the puddle, he could still be lying here. I checked his pulse. I started to walk out, but had to step out of my shoes because they were all sticky and I didn't want to track the goo all over. I had just started to dial 911 when I heard Mother and ran up the stairs to stop her from coming down."

"Let's do it."

As Daisy got to the top of the stairs she slapped her forehead. "I didn't use my phone to call. I used Mother's! When I saw what I thought was Sophia standing there at the top of the steps, I freaked out and dropped it over the railing. I remember hearing it land on the basement floor. Rats, I'll bet the police have it."

"And it's probably broken."

"Better not be. I paid a fortune for it. According to the ad I could throw that baby out of the Washington Monument and still use it to call my lawyer right after I got arrested for littering from a height."

"Well, now you have an excuse to call Brian. There's nothing else to do here, so let's go. It's unnerving and I'm in need of pizza."

As they were leaving Daisy reset the alarm. They stepped outside and she carefully reattached the tape. "I'm getting good at this."

Rose looked around. "Great. Hurry before someone shows up and wants to know why you're re-taping the door."

"Nobody's showing up. It's just you, me and this spooky old house. Come on."

"Where are we going?"

"Just looking around. I want to see if that glowy stuff is anywhere outside. I was thinking about it being in the cellar. I know it was there and I wonder if that was part of Wally's plan to catch the intruder."

"Well, if it was, it worked. Or rather the intruder caught him. But why would Wally do that? From what you've told me, he was the last person on earth who would deface that house."

Daisy thought a minute. "So maybe Wally didn't put

it there. Maybe the burglar did. And if he did, we should find out why."

"I don't think we should do that. I think we should get out of here. Besides, I don't see anything glowing. Do you?"

"No. You're right. Let's go."

As they turned to go Daisy grabbed Rose's arm. "Look. In the trees."

Rose whispered, "Great Caesar's galloping ghost! What is that?" A candle flame flickered as it moved through the thicket behind the outbuildings.

"I'm pretty sure it's Sophia."

The flame went out as it got near the old kitchen. Rose said, "Wow!"

"I told you. So now do you believe me?"

"What I believe is that a man was killed here the other night and we are standing around in the dark watching some nut carry a candle through the woods. And what I really believe is that we should get the heck out of Dodge - now!"

Rose started off, but Daisy said, "Wait a sec. I want to check out the kitchen. I think Sophia might have been pointing us toward it."

Before Rose could stop her Daisy trotted the thirty feet to the dependency and disappeared around the back. She returned half a minute later waving something in the air. "I knew it! I found something important."

"A silver goblet?"

"You wish." She shined her flashlight on a scrap of paper. "No. This little piece of paper. It was caught in the hinge of the cellar door. I'm not sure what it is." She shoved it in her pocket. "But I'm pretty sure it's a clue."

"Of course it is. Happy now? Let's go."

But as they were leaving Rose stopped dead in her tracks and said, "Did you hear that?"

"What?"

"Sammy Davis, Jr."

"I didn't hear anything. What are you talking about?"

"I hope nothing at all."

They picked up a pizza from Ledo's on their way home. The car ride was unusually quiet. Daisy was examining her find. Rose was deep in thought.

As they pulled up in front of the house Rose said, "Why didn't we find any paint?"

"Hmm? What about paint?"

"If the paint on your dress was from the cellar and there isn't any sign of it down there now..."

Daisy's stomach lurched as she stared at her sister. "Then somebody must have been there and cleaned it off while I was calling the police."

Chapter Eight

The land line was ringing as Daisy ran in the door. She grabbed it and shouted, "Hello!"

"Daisy? This is Brian Hathaway. Is everything all right? You sound upset."

"Sorry. I just walked in." In a quieter tone she said, "Hello, Detective Hathaway. How may I be of service?"

"I was calling to let you know I have your cell phone."

"Well, isn't this a coincidence? I was just going to call you and see if, by any chance, you found it. Can I have it back or do you need it for evidence or something?"

"No. You can have it back. I just need to know why it was in the cellar."

"And I can tell you why. I've been going crazy to figure out where I left it, so Rose and I were just retracing my steps."

"Were you?"

"Yes, we were. Figuratively, of course. And I remembered that I dropped it down the stairs when my mother scared the bejabbers out of me."

"Your mother scared you?"

"Well, yes. She'd have scared you, too. Dressed up like Sophia's ghost right after I had found poor Wally – well, I jumped about thirteen feet and I dropped my phone. So I used Mother's to call 911. Is mine all in one piece, by any chance?"

"It is. I thought I might bring it by."

"Oh, sure. I'll be here with bells on. Well, not actually

with bells on. That's just an expression and I don't know why I said it."

He laughed. "I'll be there in half an hour."

Daisy hung up.

Rose shook her head and said, "How may I be of service? You'll be here with bells on? That was the best you could come up with?"

"Apparently. I seem to turn into a babbling idiot every time I talk to that man."

Half an hour later Rose had cocktails ready to go. The pizza was warming in the oven and Daisy was pacing the floor. Rose said, "Stop that. You're making me crazy."

Daisy went to the desk and stared at the fragment of paper lying on it. "I think it's part of a map. Look. It could be the grounds of Holly Hill."

Rose picked it up. "Why? It's just a bunch of squiggles."

"Those aren't squiggles. Look at it. It's got a little compass rose and I'll bet that's the mansion, so that other square must be the kitchen."

Rose looked at it closely. "Okay. I guess it could be the kitchen. I mean, you found it right there. The paper looks old. What do you think those little dotted lines are? Walkways?"

"I don't know. We know there was a path from the old kitchen to the east door, but nothing going to the back of the house."

"Maybe there was a long time ago."

"No, I don't think so. There was really no actual exit on that side, just a veranda and a walled garden. There was no gate in it. But I'm going to research this. Those dots must mean something."

"Miss Utility? Someone planning on digging up the yard?"

"Rose, you're not taking this seriously, are you?"

The doorbell rang. Daisy said, "Should I tell Brian about this? No. I can't. Then I'd have to tell him we were at the mansion tonight."

"Oh, what a tangled web we weave…"

"Rose, you know that you are no help at all."

"I do my best."

"Well, don't. I won't mention the map yet since we don't even know if it means anything. But I should probably mention the paint." She shoved the paper into the desk drawer.

A minute later Daisy led Brian Hathaway up the stairs. She was chattering on about how dark the night was, that she must be getting old because she now had trouble seeing at night sometimes when driving, and that she had heard there are special glasses for that very problem.

Finally, Rose shoved a glass into her hand. "Try this. I call it a Babbling Idiot." She handed another to Brian and took one for herself. "Cheers!"

Daisy seemed to deflate suddenly. "I am so sorry. You seem to make me very nervous for some reason. Maybe because you're a policeman."

"Weren't you married to a cop?"

"Yes, I was."

"Did he make you nervous?"

"No. He just made me want to smack him in the head. But we won't go there."

"Fine with me." He handed her the phone. "I found it this evening when I was going through the evidence bags. Marc called you."

"How do you know?"

"I answered the call. That's how I found out the phone was yours."

"Did he leave a message?"

"No. Just said, "Figures," after I identified myself and

then he hung up."

Daisy nodded. "Good. Let's have pizza."

They had finished the pizza and salad and Rose was pouring tea to go with coffee cake. "Can you talk about the murder? Do you know when he was killed? Adele Long, the woman who lives there in the Dower House, is a good friend and Daisy and I are worried about her."

"We're pretty sure he'd been dead about eight hours. And I talked to Ms. Long. She's a little strange, isn't she? She said she wasn't worried, that Sophia would keep an eye on her. At least her nephew was there and said he'd look after her. And she has an alarm system, but says she rarely turns it on. I did check her locks and windows. They're pretty solid. And I've made sure someone will drive by Ms. Long's house at least once an hour."

Daisy said, "That's good. But do you have any leads?"

"That I really can't talk about."

"Well, have you seen any ghosts? You could talk about that."

"No. No ghosts."

"How about paint? Did you find any paint?"

"Why would we? What kind of paint?"

Daisy took a deep breath. "Well, I seem to have gotten some weird kind of paint on the dress I was wearing. And I really think the only place I could have gotten it on there was at the mansion on Friday. So, I just wondered if you or your guys found any damp paint."

"No. We didn't find anything like that." He got up and took his dishes to the kitchen. "It's late. I'm afraid I've got to get going."

Daisy walked him to the door. He said, "You've fed me twice now. It's time I returned the favor. How about dinner Friday?"

She smiled. "Dinner sounds good. I'd like that."

As they were cleaning the kitchen Rose said, "Babbling or not, somehow you're making a good impression."

"I am, aren't I? I can't believe he checked to see if I'm married."

"Well, that could be because you're a suspect. You *did* find the body! And you were practically incoherent when he interviewed you."

"He wouldn't ask me out if I were a suspect." Daisy put the last of the dishes into the washer. "Would he?"

"Why not? That way he can put you off your guard and pounce when you give yourself away."

"Rose, that's not funny. Do you really think that's why he asked me out?"

"Of course not. I think he's smitten!"

Refusing to bow down to the 24/7 retail school of thought, Champagne Taste was closed on Sundays. Daisy was up early. She had already fed the animals, made scones and was sipping her second cup of tea when Rose came down at eight o'clock.

Daisy said, "Wow. You look nice. Where are you off to?" Rose was wearing a new black cashmere turtleneck, grey wool slacks and high heeled boots.

"Peter and I are going to Harper's Ferry to look at leaves."

"Well, good as they look, I'd switch the boots. That's a heck of a hill they've got up there."

"Rats! Why is it always a choice between looking good and being able to walk?" She ran back upstairs and came down moments later in jeans and Uggs. "At least I can still wear the sweater."

Peter got there at nine and off they went to enjoy the beauty of the Blue Ridge Mountains in October. Daisy yawned and settled down in her recliner with the Sunday crossword. Roscoe sauntered into the room, leapt onto the desk, and knocked the Ouija board onto the floor.

Daisy asked, "Just what do you think you're doing?"

The cat pushed the box across the room to her. Daisy looked at him curiously. "You want to talk to a dead guy?"

Roscoe just sat on the box and purred. "Okay. But I need someone else. I've read that it's very dangerous to use the Board alone." Roscoe yowled. "Yes, I know you're here, but I'm pretty sure the directions referred to people. I'll see what Mother's up to this afternoon."

Angela was, of course, up for anything in the realm of the paranormal. "I'll bring the wine."

As they were setting up the table and lighting candles Angela said, "Thank God you called. I needed to get out of my house. Your father shows up at all hours and asks me out to dinner or a movie. The man has never sat through an entire movie in his life! I can't think what's gotten into him."

"Me, either. His showing up like this is just weird."

They heard paw steps on the back stairs. Malcolm and Percy trotted in and hopped up on the empty chair. Roscoe planted himself on the edge of the table. When they had all settled themselves at the table, Daisy sipped her wine and said, "Who shall we summon?"

A man's voice boomed out, "Lydia, of course. We were interrupted the other day. I want to call her back." Dick Forrest appeared in the kitchen doorway.

Daisy jumped a foot out of her chair. "Dad! You have to stop just letting yourself in. And for the love of Pete start wearing shoes I can hear on the steps!"

Angela stood up and thundered, "What the hell are you doing here? I can't get away from you for ten minutes. Did you follow me? That's called stalking. It's a crime."

"You two aren't making me feel very welcome," he said as he pulled up a chair. "Your manners need a little work. I thought I'd drop in on my daughters on a beautiful Sunday afternoon. That's not a crime, is it?"

Angela closed her eyes, placed her fingertips on her clavicle, and took a deep breath. "I am centered. I am calm."

Dickie said, "Well then, let's get this party started. Where's Rose?"

"Out for the day." Daisy sat back down and asked, "Mother, are you all right?"

"Of course, I am. I'll ignore him. I am centered. I am calm. I will call Lydia. Maybe she will tell him to get lost."

Dickie poked her arm. "Angie, you know you still have feelings for me."

She looked at him and said, "You're right. I do. And that's the problem. I still feel like killing you. But that is bad for my soul, so I'll pretend you're not here."

She sipped her wine, lit the final candle, and placed her fingertips on the pointer. Daisy joined her. So did Dick. Angela intoned, "Ouija, Ouija, are you there?"

They waited a moment and the little piece of wood started moving. YES.

She continued, "Is Lydia there? Lydia Forrest, are you there?"

YES.

Dickie started to ask a question, but Angela smacked his hand away from the pointer and said, "You are a guest. No questions." He put his fingers back and they waited.

"Lydia, this is Angela. Are you all right?"
YES.
"Do you need anything?"
YES.

"Can I help?"

R E B O N C J L E

Daisy said, "What does that mean?"

"I think that B was a C. And the J could have been an I." Dickie was jotting down the letters. "That would spell 'reconcile'."

Angela tried again. "Well that ridiculous. I can't believe Lydia has to reconcile with anyone. Lydia, we don't understand."

The pointer started moving again. F O R G I V E D I C K I E

"Look! She wants you to forgive me! Lydia is telling us that we should be together." Dickie leapt out of his chair and put his arms around Angela.

Angela nearly knocked him over as she pushed him away. "What are you doing? I think you've lost your mind. You were moving that pointer and you know it."

"I wasn't. It was Lydia. She wants us to be happy together."

"You're an idiot." She stood up and grabbed his arm. "I've had enough of you for today. Time to go."

As Angela was escorting Dickie to the door Roscoe put his paw on the pointer and it started moving. Daisy watched in fascination as it spelled out B S. "I think you hit the nail on the head, buddy. Time to put away the Ouija board and figure out what Dad's game is."

Angela came back in and said, "You don't think Lydia really wants us to get back together, do you?"

"Absolutely not. Dad was cheating - again. But why is he doing this? That's what I want to know."

Chapter Nine

"What a wonderful day!" Rose said, dropping into her recliner. "We walked and walked and shopped. Then we had a lovely dinner at a cozy little inn. Then we stopped in a pub and listened to folk music. I'm worn out. What did you guys get up to?"

"Well, Mother, the critters and I were going to play with the Ouija board, but Dad showed up and kind of ruined it." She told her sister about the afternoon. "Mother's really upset. She's afraid Lydia might actually want her to get back together with Dad."

"Daisy, you have to stop this nonsense. It's a piece of cardboard and a little wooden pointer. It has NO mystical powers and you should stop encouraging Mother."

"I don't know about no mystical powers at all. I'm sure it has some. But I'm also sure Dad was moving the thing this afternoon."

"Well, that's something, I guess."

"Maybe Lydia can straighten Mother out on Tuesday."

"Tuesday?"

"At the séance."

"Silly me. How could I forget? I'm in charge of the flowers."

"And I intend to make sure that our father will not be able to attend. I don't want him rattling chains under the table or playing ghost sounds through his phone."

"How are you going to do that?"

"I haven't figured that out yet. Maybe I'll have him arrested."

Tuesday the shop was busy from the time they opened until Rose turned the sign on the front door at six o'clock. She, Daisy and Tonya grabbed a quick bite in the kitchen before they set out for Adele's.

"Are you sure you don't mind me going with you?" Tonya asked.

Daisy said, "Of course we don't mind. Why would we?"

"Well, I kind of invited myself. But I've never been to a séance. They always sound so mystical and exciting."

"The more the merrier," said Rose. "So, you believe in this stuff, too?"

Tonya hesitated. "I like to keep an open mind. I do believe that we exist somewhere after we die. And I always feel like my Grandmother answers me in one way or another when I talk to her and she's been gone for ten years now. So, yes, I guess I do believe in this stuff."

"Well, I think this is a big waste of time. But it will make Adele and Mother happy."

"What about me?" asked Daisy. "It will make me happy, too. I want to know just what Sophia was trying to tell me!"

It was dark when they pulled into Adele's driveway and parked next to Angela's Lexus. Angela opened the front door and handed them each a flute of champagne. She eyed them critically and said, "Is this what you wear to a séance?"

Daisy and Rose were both wearing jeans. Daisy had topped hers with a mauve sweater and paisley infinity scarf. Rose had on a grey turtle neck and black blazer. Daisy said, "Pretty much."

Looking at Angela in a brown monk's robe with the cowl pulled over her hair Rose asked, "We're not meeting a coven or something, are we?"

Angela sighed loudly and said, "I sometimes despair of both of you. Tonya, that gold tunic is perfect. You look lovely."

The small living room seemed to be overflowing with people. Lolita Llewelyn was sitting on the couch next Leo Walters. Peter Fleming was standing by the fireplace with an amused look on his face. Adele in her flowing purple caftan was lighting candles and incense. She said, "Daisy, Rose, it's so good of you to come. And Tonya, it's so good to see you. It's been too long."

Rose handed her the flowers. "Perfect."

Leo walked over to Daisy. "I hear this is your idea, Daisy. The séance?"

"Not entirely mine."

"Well, as long you are doing this, maybe you can get someone from the other side to convince Aunt Adele to come stay with me until this murderer is caught. She absolutely refuses." He adjusted his glasses and looked at Adele.

"You fuss too much. I'm fine," said Adele. "There is nothing here anyone could want and I'm not planning on skulking around the mansion. Wally Stone was unwise to take matters into his own hands. I'm sorry he's dead, but only an idiot would plan to catch a burglar without anyone to help."

"I don't know, Adele. We don't know what the thief was looking for. If it was Sophia's silver, he or she might think you have it," said Rose.

Peter asked, "Adele, do you think there really is a hidden treasure?" Adele sipped her champagne and smiled.

Rose glanced at Peter. "Thank you for coming."

"I wouldn't miss it."

"Where is Marc? He seemed so eager to be here," asked Angela.

"Yes. Where is Marc?" echoed Rose. "He's usually first on board for anything that could be construed as dubious in nature."

Daisy smiled. "I gave him a little assignment. I had to promise him a full accounting of the evening and, of course, dinner to get him to do it. But it will be worth it."

Rose looked at her quizzically for a moment. Then she laughed out loud and said, "Good thinking."

Angela was about to ask what they were talking about when Adele said, "If we're all here, I think we should start. Let's move to the dining room."

It was a good-sized room, but with a Sheraton sideboard on one wall, a longcase clock in the corner, and an oval mahogany table with eight chairs around it, it was a bit crowded.

A large mirror over the sideboard reflected the dancing flames of the candles as they shone eerily on the black marble lion and the copper urn that sat on it. A window on the opposite wall that looked out over the back garden into the darkness of the trees beyond.

Lolita sat at the head of the table looking every bit the medium in her long black dress, silk scarves draped around her neck and waist, large gold hoops in her ears. The candles flickered and the smell of patchouli permeated the air. A wind chime outside the window tinkled gently in some unseen breeze.

Adele said, "Everyone, please have a seat. Leo, turn out the lights."

They sat down and looked at Lolita expectantly. She closed her eyes, raised her hands, palms up, and said, "Please join hands. We have come tonight in the name of peace and goodwill to communicate with the spirit of Sophia Long."

A sudden gust of wind rattled the window and the

chimes rang wildly for a moment and then stopped altogether. The room was silent except for the ticking of the old clock - one minute, two minutes. Lolita opened her eyes and looked at each of them. "There are spirits here, but I feel unrest."

Rose whispered, "Well, I do too, now. This is spooky!"

Daisy kicked her. "Ssh!"

Someone coughed.

Lolita continued, "We come together in a spirit of goodwill. Our minds are cleared of doubt and anger. We ask to speak to Sophia Long." She closed her eyes and asked, "Sophia, are you here?" She tilted her head to one side and said, "Someone is here."

The wind chimes rang softly. Lolita's voice dropped an octave. "It is not Sophia. Who are you? Josiah? Josiah Long is here." The candles flickered.

"I'll bet he knows where the silver is. Ask him," said Daisy.

"Is there something you wish to tell us?" Lolita shuddered, "I feel only anger and malice. Josiah, we have come as friends. You are not welcome if you cannot join us in harmony." Everyone was still as they watched Lolita slowly shake her head back and forth mouthing, "Leave us, leave us, leave us."

"He's gone. I don't feel anyone... Wait! The children are here. Sophia's children are here." She cocked her head again as if listening. "I think they are searching. They are sad and afraid, but they are silent. I'm sorry. They've gone."

She dropped her hands into her lap and sighed. Suddenly she raised her hands again. "Someone else has come. Sophia? Is it Sophia?" The lights in the room flickered on and off, then on and off again. Daisy whispered, "It must be Sophia. Adele says she loves electricity." The others sat still and waited.

Lolita sat quietly, listening. "Sophia says that there is evil here. No. Not evil, but danger. There is danger near one of you. Great care must be taken. The silver is cursed. Murder has been done before. Murder may be done again."

Daisy looked around the table. "Who is she warning?"

Adele answered, "I believe Sophia is speaking to me."

"Yes, Adele. She feels you are in danger. Sophia wants to send you a message. I don't understand. It's confused." Lolita sat in silence for a long moment, then opened her eyes and said, "She's gone. I couldn't make out what she was trying to say. I think Josiah's presence upset her."

"Can we call her again? Or maybe call the children?" asked Daisy.

"I'm sorry, they've gone and I'm quite tired."

After a few moments, Leo got up and turned on the lights. Daisy stretched her arms and said, "I feel like I just woke up."

Beside her Rose sat still, her eyes closed, her breathing soft. "Rose fell asleep."

Lolita said, "Be very gentle. She may be in a trance. Sometimes spirits visit others at the table."

"Oh, that's silly. Rose doesn't even believe in this stuff." She shook her sister's shoulder. "Come on, Rose. Wakey, wakey, eggs and bakey."

Rose opened her eyes with a start and said in a sing-song voice, "Beware, beware, beware."

"Rose wake up." Daisy shook her again. "Why are you saying beware? Beware of what?"

Rose shrugged her shoulders and yawned. "Hmm? I don't know. Just beware."

"Well, it would certainly help if you were a bit more specific."

Suddenly the lion on the buffet fell on its side. They all jumped. Daisy said, "Who did that?"

Rose gasped. "The lion! She said, 'Beware the lion.'"

"Who said?" asked Daisy.

"I think it was Sophia."

"Well, doesn't that just take the Angel Food. Why didn't she tell me? What kind of ghost switches sisters in mid-stream? Rose doesn't even believe she exists! I have to say, I am a little miffed. And what does that mean anyway? What's a lion got to do with any of this? Ooh, unless he's not marble and is really silver and was made by Paul Revere!"

Just as she put her hand out to examine the statue, a billow of mist rolled into the room through the doorway. It was so thick they could barely see one another.

Rose whispered, "Holy London fog!" Daisy murmured, "I told you." They all stood in stunned silence as it filled the room and then slowly disappeared through the closed window.

Tonya, closest to the window, stared after it in disbelief. The mist was rolling into the trees, but was still thick on the lawn when she saw a small light bobbing through it. It seemed to be heading straight toward the house. As it got closer she could see a shadowy figure in black that appeared to be holding it. Tonya shrieked and grabbed Angela's arm. She whispered, "Is that Josiah?".

Suddenly, the figure loomed up in the window and a voice boomed out, "Did I miss it?"

Angela peered back and said, "Dickie?"

"Who else were you expecting?"

"You idiot! You scared us half to death."

"Let me in. It's getting cold out here. And this fog is pretty damp."

"Adele, I am so sorry about this, but I know he won't

go away."

"Of course, let the man in." She turned to her nephew. "Leo, dear, I have a pitcher of rather nice Kentucky Corpse Revivers ready on a tray in the kitchen. Would you mind bringing it in? I thought we might need something stronger than coffee."

Settled in the living room drinks in hand, Rose took a sip. "Pretty tasty, the perfect après séance pick-me-up."

Dickie downed his drink in one gulp and said, "Well, did you get through to anyone? Did you make contact with Lydia?"

Lolita started to answer, but Daisy cut her off. "He really doesn't need to know."

"Of course, I need to know. Lydia wants to tell your mother something important."

Daisy sighed loudly. "Dad, where's Marc?"

"I left him parking the car up at the mansion."

The front door opened and Marc Proctor stuck his head in. "Mind if I join you?" He sidled into the room looking sheepish as Daisy introduced him to Adele and Leo.

She squinted at him and said, "Marc?"

"Sorry. I tried, but I couldn't stop him."

"You drove him over here!"

Dickie said, "Don't blame the boy. He did his best. He took me to dinner and then dragged me back to his shop to look at an antique Ouija board which he had trouble finding once we got there. By that time, I figured out what was going on. I have to say I'm a little sad that my own daughter would set me up like that."

"Oh, really! Dickie, you need to grow up." Angela crossed her arms. "It's more than a bit annoying that you think you can just barge in on things that are none of your business."

Adele held up her hand and said, "It makes no

matter. I think this evening gave us quite a lot to think about and I'm rather tired."

Rose got up. "You're right, Adele. It's time we got out of your hair. Come along, children. We'll figure this out in the light of day. Peter, come back with me. We'll have a nightcap."

Leo walked out with Daisy. "I'm worried about my aunt. She won't let me stay here with her."

"I'm not sure what I can do about that."

"I'm not either, but could we get together and talk about it? I really think we need to do something to protect her, especially after tonight's warning."

"Of course. How about lunch tomorrow at our place?"

Chapter Ten

"Now do you believe in ghosts?" Daisy asked as she scooped tea into a teapot and filled it with boiling water the next morning.

"I wouldn't go that far. But I have to admit something strange was going on."

"Strange? That's all you've got to say? Fog filled rooms, statues tipping over for no reason, and sing-song voices – coming out of your mouth I might add – and you just think it's strange? You're nuts. We had an encounter with the other side!"

"Perhaps."

"And what do you think 'beware the lion' means?"

"I don't know. Maybe there's a clue in that statue or under it – in the sideboard."

"A clue to what? The murder or the missing silver?" Daisy sipped her tea. "I think we need to find out just what it all means. After all, Sophia came to us for help. By the way, Leo's coming for lunch. He's worried about Adele."

"He should be. I am too. There's a murderer running around and that séance certainly didn't make me feel like she's any safer. But do you know what is really bothering me? Dad! Why is he always showing up where he's not invited? And this sudden interest he has in the occult is too odd! Not to mention his interest in us."

"Rose, you certainly don't think he murdered anyone, do you? Dad's just trying to get Mother's attention for some reason."

"I don't think he killed Wally. I can't see any connection he would have with the mansion, but I think he's been snooping around up there. I didn't tell you this before, but the night we broke into the mansion to get your phone…"

"We didn't break in. I had the key!"

"Okay. The night we *didn't* break into the mansion…"

"What about it?"

"If you would shut up for one second, I'll tell you."

"You don't have to be snippy."

Rose took a sip of tea. "I think I heard Dad's phone."

"When?"

"Right after you ran off by yourself and found that little piece of trash. Just as we were leaving I heard Sammy Davis Jr. singing."

Daisy smacked her forehead. "It wasn't trash. It was a map. And I'm glad you reminded me. I'd almost forgotten about it. I need to do some research."

"Daisy, I don't care about a scrap of paper. I care about the fact that I heard Sammy Davis, Jr. singing."

"I didn't hear anything."

"Well, I did."

"Even if you did, it didn't have to be our father's phone."

Rose looked at her sister. "How many lunatics out there have that ringtone?" She sighed. "Maybe I am wrong. Maybe I just imagined it."

"I think you did – imagine it, I mean. At any rate, we've got work to do before Leo gets here. So let's move it!"

Daisy was just taking the Chicken Divan out of the oven when Leo Walters rang the doorbell. "Leo, come in and make yourself at home. I've just got to toss the salad. Rose is in the shop getting Tonya squared away. She'll be here in a minute."

"Can I help with something? That smells pretty good."

"Thanks. You could open the wine. It's on the table."

As he was opening the bottle Roscoe walked into the dining room, sniffed Leo's shoe, and leapt onto the top shelf of the bookcase where he settled down to watch the proceedings.

Leo said, "That's a beautiful cat."

Daisy smiled fondly at the golden tabby. "He is, isn't he? Well, everything's ready. Let me call Rose."

Leo sat back in his chair, pulled an orange cloth out of his pocket and started cleaning his glasses and said, "That was delicious. Thank you. I know I shouldn't be bothering you with this, but I know you care about Adele. The problem is I don't know how to help her. She refuses to let me stay with her. She won't stay with me. She's all alone out there with ghosts, thieves, and murderers searching for the silver."

Rose asked, "So you think Wally was killed by somebody after the silver?"

"What else could it be? From what you tell me Wally was probably lying in wait trying to catch the intruder when he was killed." He shook his head. "Whoever it was had to be after something they thought was worth killing for and the silver is the only thing I can think of. What else would someone break into the mansion to get? That tea set has taken on a life of its own. Crazies are always contacting Adele and asking if they can hunt for it."

"I didn't know that. Anybody lately?" asked Daisy.

"A couple of calls from history buffs who just wanted to look around. But she did get a strange call around the end of August from someone who said he was an archeologist from the Maryland Historical Society. He insisted that there were tunnels on the estate, possibly to do with the Underground Railroad, and he wanted to do a proper dig on the property. Of course, Adele told him that was ridiculous."

Rose said, "Did she get his name?"

"Yes. He called himself Howard Carter and told her he studied at University of Sheffield in England. When she asked for his phone number, he just said he'd call later when she had had time to think about it."

"Well, that does sound a sketchy. Howard Carter! And tunnels?" asked Daisy thoughtfully. "I've never heard of any tunnels."

"That's because there aren't any. Just like there isn't any silver."

Daisy poured some more tea. "What do you think happened to it?"

Leo thought a minute. "I don't know. And there's no one to ask, no family, I mean. Adele and I are the only ones left. I wish there were silver hidden somewhere on the estate. I could really use that money. But as far as I know it's long gone."

Rose asked, "I thought Sophia and Josiah had a lot of children."

"They had five, but only three made it to adulthood - Ambrose Henry, my great-great-great grandfather; his sister Amelia who never had children; and his sister, Matilda, the black sheep of the family."

"Black sheep! What did she do?"

"When she was sixteen she eloped with a man named Louis Sutter without her brother's consent. He refused to acknowledge them and she and her husband eventually moved to England. Ambrose prohibited all contact with her. Apparently, Louis Sutter was a pretty bad guy, or at least Ambrose thought so. I think Aunt Adele might know more than she lets on. But she just clams up anytime I ask her about the family."

Rose said, "So no family journals or diaries still in existence? And no long-lost cousins?"

"Not that I'm aware of. At least, if there are any Meade-Long relatives out there somewhere, they've never been in contact with us. But this doesn't get us any closer on how to protect my aunt. I really think I should be there with her, but she won't have it."

"I have a thought about that," said Daisy. "I'm going to talk to Mother. If anyone can get Adele to see sense, she can."

After Leo left Daisy got out the little scrap of paper she had found and put it on the dining room table. She studied it for a long time. "Look at this, Rose."

"What?"

"What if there are tunnels on the mansion grounds and that's what the dotted lines represent?"

"Daisy, I think you're a teabag short of a pot."

"I'm serious, Rose. What if there are?"

"That's ridiculous. If there were any tunnels they would have been found by now."

"Not necessarily. I don't think there has ever been an archaeological dig on the property. At least, there aren't any records of one. Suppose they were built when the mansion was built, but kept secret. Who'd know?"

"If they were secret, where did that map come from?"

Daisy picked up the scrap and stared at it. "Good question. Who would know?"

"Sophia and her lion friend, no doubt."

"I don't think 'beware the lion' sounds like a friend." Daisy frowned and bit her lip.

Rose asked, "What?"

"A relative would know. Leo means lion, doesn't it?"

Rose looked at her sister and said, "Yes. It does."

Rose was turning the sign on the shop door to CLOSED when she saw an old grey clunker pull up to the curb and Angela get out clutching Percy in one arm and a tote bag in the other. She held the door open for her mother. "I didn't know you were coming over."

"I was at a loose end and I knew Daisy would be out with Brian, so I thought we could go to dinner."

"Sure, that would be nice. What's with the car?"

Angela smiled. "It's my Rent-a-Wreck."

"Hmm. Your Rent-a-Wreck? Somehow I get the feeling that dinner's not the only thing on the menu."

Angela put Percy in the backyard while Rose closed out the register and locked up for the night. Finally, she turned the key to the connecting hallway door and they went up to the apartment.

"Okay, Mother, I know you weren't at a loose end. What are we really doing this evening?"

"Well, actually we are going to follow your father. I happen to know he's meeting someone for dinner tonight at Rip's Country Inn. I want to know who and why."

"How do you know he's meeting someone?"

"I overheard him when he was at the house."

"Dad was at your house?"

"Yes. I told you he seems to be stalking me and I want to know why. He lurks. Every time I turn around, there he is asking me out. Dinner, a movie, dancing. And last night he practically forced his way into the house – you know how he is – and when I went to the kitchen to get the carving knife…"

"Mother, you didn't threaten him with a knife, did you?"

"Of course not. It was for the pumpkin. But if he took it as an invitation to leave that was fine with me. Anyway, I overheard him talking to someone and he mentioned Holly Hill. And then he made a date to meet this someone tonight at Rip's at seven-thirty. I intend to be there."

"Hence the old car. I see. But, Mother, don't you think he'll recognize us when we get out of it?"

Angela positively beamed. "Wait till you see what I have in this bag. Tada!" She pulled out two wigs, two pairs of fake glasses, and a bundle of old clothes.

Rose held a sweater up and said, "We aren't really going to put these on, are we?"

"Yes. We are. They blend with the background. Your father would never look twice at someone wearing that charming, though rather baggy, pea green sweater, would he?"

"It's got a hole in it."

"So it does. All the better. Do you want to be ash blond or daring red?"

"Holy shades of Lucy and Ethel. This is silly."

"Well, it might seem silly, but it will work. I want to know what he's up to."

Rose sighed and picked up the blond wig. "I do, too. Okay, I'll be Ethel." She looked at the clock. "You said 7:30? We'd better move it if we want to be there before Dad arrives."

Chapter Eleven

Decked out in their wigs, fake glasses, and ghastly clothing Rose and Angela pulled into the restaurant's parking lot and eased into a spot at the far edge. "We'll wait here until Dickie shows up and then follow him in. If it's not too crowded tonight, we can get the booth right next to them. Then if we're very quiet we can eavesdrop and hear what's going on. If not, I'll use my back-up."

Rose glanced at herself in the mirror. "This wig itches. It is new, isn't it? I'm not wearing something you found by the side of the road, am I?"

"Ssh. There he is."

Dickie Forrest got out of a bright red Mustang and looked around the parking lot. At the same time, another man got out of a car several spots away and walked over to him. They shook hands and went into the inn.

Angela snapped a picture of the two and said, "So he's not meeting a woman. I wonder who that is."

Rose shook her head. "Mother, is that why we're here? You thought he had a date?"

"Well, I did wonder. He keeps asking me out and I don't know why. And I know I can't trust him, so when I heard him set this up I just wanted to see who it was with. Anyway, let's go."

They got out of the car. Rose saw her reflection in the window and said, "We look like a couple of underpaid bag ladies."

"Nit-picking is not attractive," Angela said as she opened the restaurant door.

Rip's was a long-standing fixture in the adjoining town of Bowie that hearkened back to the glory days of horse racing in the area. Inside, the high-sided booths resembling horse stalls were dimly lit and intimate – good for a romantic dinner or spying on someone without being seen.

They were just in time to see the maître d' lead Dickie and his friend to *Secretariat's* stall. "Perfect. Luck is with us. *Dancer's Image* right next to them is empty. I'll ask for that."

They slid into their booth and Angela started fiddling with her phone. Then she pulled a roll of duct tape from her bag.

Rose asked, "What are you doing?"

"Ssh. Whisper. I don't want you-know-who to hear us. This is my back-up, in case we can't hear. I'm going tape this to the top of the booth and record what they're saying."

"You certainly came prepared. What if we couldn't get this booth?"

"I figured I'd pay a waiter to do this for me."

"Right! Are we going to whisper all night?"

"No. We're not going to talk at all. How can we hear them if we're talking?"

The waiter came by, introduced himself, offered them menus, and asked if they would like a drink to start. Rose started to answer, but Angela kicked her shin and quickly got out a small pad of paper and wrote something. She handed it to Ben, the waiter, and he said, "I'm so sorry to hear that. Just write down what you'd like and I'll get it right away."

She jotted something down and he said, "Absolutely," and went off in the direction of the bar.

Rose said, "Mother, what was that?"

"I told him we both were suffering from laryngitis and couldn't talk. I ordered us iced tea. We have to keep a clear head."

Moments later they overheard Dickie and his friend order drinks. Dickie's voice boomed, "I'll have a Zombie."

Angela sniffed. "A Zombie! He should be a zombie. What an idiot and he's driving. If he's tiddly when he leaves here, I'm calling Tom Willis and telling him to track Dickie down." She leaned back against the side of the booth. "I wish I could hear that other man. I hope the phone is picking him up."

"I thought we weren't supposed to be talking!"

"Oops. You're right."

They finished their meal in something like silence. Even so, they couldn't hear much of the conversation next door. After practically shouting his order, Dickie's voice sunk to a conversational level and they could only pick up the odd word here and there. His friend, they couldn't hear at all. When Dickie ordered coffee, Angela got the waiters attention and paid their bill. She and Rose sidled out.

Rose said, "Well, that was just pretty dumb. Now what?"

"I want you to wait by the door and loiter while I get the car. As soon as you see them walk out, you run in and un-tape the phone and get back out here. I'll have the car at the door, so we can follow him."

"Why didn't you bring the phone when we left?"

"They might be making plans. Stop complaining and loiter. With your back to the door so Dickie can't see you face. And hunch your shoulders a bit. You have such an elegant posture that he might recognize you."

Rose smiled. "Do I? Thanks."

"Loiter!"

Rose loitered. She was had just gotten in place,

adjusted her wig which had slipped sideways a bit and hunched her shoulders when the two men emerged. As she slipped into the doorway she heard the Dickie say, "Great to see you again, Len."

It was busy at the reception desk and she was able to edge her way past the knot of people crowding the inner doorway and get to their booth. A young couple was sitting there enjoying Strawberry Margaritas.

She said, "Ooh, those are tasty, aren't they? And I highly recommend the shrimp. If you'll just excuse me, I forgot my phone. It's taped right back there. So easy to lose," as she reached over the startled woman and tore the phone off the top of the seat. Unfortunately, her wig fell off as she did this and landed on a bread plate. "Oops! I guess I should tape this on too." Rose grabbed the wig and ran out the door.

Angela was waiting in front waving frantically. Rose got in and they tore out of the parking lot. Angela said, "I thought we were going to lose him, but luckily he and that man kept talking. Now keep an eye on that car." They followed him as he headed north on Crain Highway, then watched as he made the right onto Defense Highway heading toward Annapolis.

Rose wondered, "Where is he going? And what's with the muscle car?"

"Is that what you call it? I don't know. Maybe he's going through male menopause. At least it makes him easy to follow."

"I think there's something more going on than male menopause. I just wish I knew what."

They followed him at a distance as he meandered through the darkened countryside finally pulling into a gated neighborhood just south of Annapolis. They could see him hold up a small card and wave to the attendant.

Angela swore mildly under her breath as she pulled

up, smiled at the young woman, and held up her own entrance pass.

Rose said, "I don't believe this," as they watched Dickie pull to a stop half a block from Angela's own home.

Angela quickly turned a corner before he saw them and stopped the car. "I told you he was stalking me! I wonder how he got that pass."

"You didn't give it to him?"

"Heavens no. And I don't know why it hasn't occurred to me sooner that he must have one."

She and Rose got out and walked through her neighbor's yard and hid behind a huge stand of pampas grass where they could watch Dickie's movements.

Angela lived in a secure upscale community for the over-55. Her home was a lovely little, two story bungalow that sat twenty feet from the street. The detached garage on the right was connected to the house by a short, covered walkway that also opened into the fenced backyard abutting the neighborhood pond. Beds of chrysanthemum lined the rear fence, hedges lined the adjoining yards, and a beautiful red maple stood in the center, now in late autumn crowned by the last of its scarlet leaves.

They watched as Dickie got out of his car, pulled on a dark hoodie, and started down the street toward the house.

Rose whispered, "He is stalking you!"

"Well, he's a lousy stalker. I'm not even home!"

He was carrying a black tote bag and what looked like a small bucket. As he went through the walkway into the backyard the motion sensor lights came on.

"What the heck is he doing in my backyard?" They waited for about ten minutes and Angela was just about to march over and confront him when Dickie reappeared and slinked off to his car.

Rose asked, "What now? Do you want to follow him again?"

"No. I want to see what he was doing back there."

They crouched down as the Mustang turned around and drove out of sight toward the gate. Angela led the way into the backyard and stood, hands on hips, staring. "Well, that's just peculiar." Nothing seemed to be out of order. Flowers, hedge, tree all looked normal. There were no weird gnomes, no toilet paper streaming from the tree, no hastily planted flowers.

Rose looked thoughtfully at the tree. "Hmmm. Let's go inside."

Angela looked at her daughter and said, "Good idea. I think this development calls for a little something to drink."

A few moments after they entered the house the motion sensor lights went out. Rose went to the kitchen, whipped up a vodka tonic and handed it to her mother as she glanced out the rear window. Angela said, "You're not drinking?"

"Not right now. Turn off the lights a minute."

"Why?"

"I'm testing a theory."

"All right. They're off. Anything?"

"No. Nothing." She stared into the night and chewed a fingernail. "Let's go into your bedroom." Angela's master bedroom was upstairs at the back of the house. She said, "Why?"

"Still testing."

Angela flipped the light switch as they went in, but Rose turned it off again. She pulled the curtains apart and said, "Holy maple syrup! I was right. Look. You can only see it in the dark and only from this angle."

Angela stared at the letters spelling FORGIVE HIM shining eerily as they dripped down the trunk.

Rose said, "What I don't get is how he thought you would see this."

"What do you mean?"

"Well, it needs to be dark to see it, but you always close your curtains at night, so you wouldn't see it, would you?"

"I do close my curtains, but I always look out at the night sky right before I get into bed. And your father knows that I do." She stared at the writing wistfully. "We did have some very good years. Maybe..."

"Maybe nothing, Mother. This is Dick Forrest we're talking about. A man who is trying to make you think a ghost wants you to forgive him. A man who's writing on trees with the same type of paint that might have been all over the mansion's basement!"

Angela looked at her daughter and straightened her shoulders. "You're right. He thinks he knows me so well. Well, it's not going to work. Just wait 'til I get my hands on him. I'll give him ghosts!" And she knocked back the vodka in one gulp and said, "You'd better drive."

They got to the Elms just as Brian Hathaway was pulling away from the curb. Daisy was standing on the porch.

Rose and Angela joined her. Rose said, "You're home early. Date didn't go well?"

Daisy smiled, "Actually it went very well, but Brian got called to a crime scene and we had to cut it short. What have you two been doing? And why are you dressed like that?"

They had left the wigs at Angela's and she had changed into her comfy sweats, but Rose still had the bag lady clothes on. "Let's get inside and we'll tell you all about our night. Then you can tell us about yours."

Daisy opened a bottle of Prosecco and Angela put

together fruit and cheese on a plate while Rose changed her clothes. She came down the stairs and said to Daisy, "You first."

"Well, there's not much to tell," said Daisy. "He took me to *Pirate's Cove* in Galesville. Our table overlooked the water. It was very romantic. I had a champagne cocktail. He had a Sam Adams. We both had Crab Imperial for dinner."

"Did he tell you about the investigation?"

"No. We didn't talk shop. We just talked about, you know, first date stuff. He told me about his ex who didn't sound too bad. Apparently, they were just very young when they got married and then they grew up and apart. No kids, though they have joint custody of Portia."

"Who is Portia if she's not his kid."

"An American Fuzzy Lop."

"A what?"

"A fuzzy white bunny who's getting on in years. He showed me her picture. She's really cute and you've got to like a guy who loves his rabbit!"

Rose said, "I guess you do. How did your end of the conversation go? Did you mention Bill at all?"

"Yes. I felt full disclosure was only fair. And I'm pretty sure I managed to talk about that cheating rat bastard I wasted so many years being married to without sounding like a lunatic. At least I think I did. I mean, he didn't run screaming out the door. I took that as a good sign and invited him to our party. We had just started this really delicious apple tart when his phone rang. Apparently, he was needed at work and he had to go. That was my night. Nothing exciting, just a nice normal evening out." She took a sip of wine, leaned back in her chair and said, "Okay, let's have it. What did you two do?"

Angela finished relating their recent adventure and

brought up the picture of Dickie and his dinner companion on her phone and handed it to Daisy.

Daisy stared at the picture. "That's Len Rutherford, the Park and Planning guy who works at the mansion. Remember, he told me he met Dad at some seminar."

"Really? I suppose it makes sense that they might meet for dinner."

"Well, what did they talk about? Could you hear?"

"Not much, but I recorded them with my phone."

Daisy looked at her. "You taped them?"

Rose nodded. "Of course, she did. And who had to look like an idiot going back into the restaurant to retrieve the phone? Me."

"Rose, don't be difficult, dear. Yes, I taped them. I thought it was best. As we found out, you just can't hear everything over the clatter of plates and other people talking."

"And you haven't listened to it yet?" asked Daisy.

"We were waiting for you, so we could all listen together." Angela pushed the PLAY button just as Daisy's cell phone rang. Daisy yanked it out and snapped, "Do you know what time it is?" She listened for a minute and said, "Brian? Oh my goodness. Of course. We'll be right over."

She hung up the phone and said, "Adele Long's been attacked."

Chapter Twelve

"How was she attacked?" asked Angela. "Where is she?"

"Brian didn't tell me anything about it except that she's at home and alone." Daisy maneuvered her car out of the garage and headed toward the mansion.

Rose said, "She's a tough old bird, Mother. I'm sure she's all right."

They pulled into Adele's driveway just as an ambulance was leaving. Brian was waiting.

"How is she?" asked Daisy. "What happened?"

"She says she's fine. It appears that she was walking around outside the mansion and somebody hit her on the head and knocked her down."

Rose said, "Oh my God! Why isn't she in the hospital?"

"Because I'm fine." Adele was standing at the far end of the porch hidden in the shadows. She was wearing a long black Chesterfield coat and a red cloth hat perched on top of what appeared to a large bird's nest of grey, black and reddish hair pieces which were listing slightly. "Now that everyone and his Great Aunt Fanny seem to be here you might as well come in."

Adele swayed a little as she opened the door. Angela took her arm and helped her out of the coat. "Sit down, Adele. Now what can I get you?"

"Nothing dear. The very nice EMT checked me and said I was fine. She told me to take two aspirin. I told her I'd call her in the morning!"

"Did you take the aspirin?"

"Not yet."

"I'll get it for you and I think, maybe, a cup of tea."

"If you're going to bother making tea, you might add a little something to it, dear. It will help me sleep."

Angela smiled and went off to find aspirin and a little something. Brian said, "Ms. Long, if you're up to it could you could just tell me what happened tonight. Then I'll get out here and let you get some rest."

"Oh me. Well, I was putting the cat out for the night and saw lights moving around outside the big house. So I slipped on my coat and hat and went up there to see if Sophia was out and about and needed my help with anything."

Daisy said, "I didn't know you had a cat." As if on cue a sleek black cat jumped into Adele's lap.

"You haven't met, have you? This is Amelia."

"Amelia? That's unusual."

"It came to me out of the blue. I found her sitting on the railing of the porch Wednesday evening and I said, 'Amelia?' and she came right to me."

"Well, she's beautiful and so friendly. We'll have to get her together with Roscoe. I think he feels left out sometimes, being the only cat."

"That would be lovely."

"Wasn't Amelia the name of Sophia's daughter?"

"Yes, dear."

Brian coughed softly as he felt the conversation getting away from him. "Could we get back to the break-in?"

"Certainly. By the time I got there the lights were gone. I walked around the house, but found no sign of Sophia or anyone else until I got to the door in the east wing. I could see a flashlight bobbing in the hall through the window.

"Well, I'd just about had it with this scoundrel.

Breaking in, killing poor Wally, and roaming all over my estate like he owns it! I banged on the door and was just about to unlock it when he came running out. He swung the door so hard, I lost my balance and it hit my head and I fell. Then the alarm started wailing. I guess that's how the police got there so quickly."

Angela walked into the room and handed Adele two little pills and a glass of water. "Take these. Tea's on its way. Were you knocked out?"

"No, I remained quite conscious. I believe it was a glancing blow, as I've heard it called it. And of course, my hat softened the impact."

Rose murmured, "Or that concoction under it." Daisy elbowed her and murmured back, "Stop that."

Adele continued, "But he very rudely lifted not one finger to help me up. I had to struggle to get to my feet. It was most undignified. I suppose it's a wonder I didn't break anything."

"Yes, it is. What were you thinking going up there by yourself in the dark? Leo's right. You shouldn't be here alone until this person is caught." Angela looked around the room. "Where is Leo, anyway? He should be here."

Brian looked up from his notebook. "I couldn't find him. No one was at his home and he wasn't answering his cell. Ms. Long, could you describe your assailant at all? Anything? Height, weight, man, woman, black, white, anything at all?"

Adele thought for a moment. "I'm sure it was a man. I'm sure he was taller than I. That's all really. I'm afraid that's not much help, is it? But it was dark. I didn't see his face or hands."

"Why do say it was a man?"

"He grunted as he swung open the door. It's very heavy. It was definitely a male grunt. But that's all that I'm sure of."

"All right, Ms. Long. We'll be back in the morning to go over the grounds and the house again. In the meantime, I've posted a man at the mansion and someone will be driving by here hourly. If you insist on staying here alone, I'd advise you not to go wandering around the grounds. And keep your alarm set."

He got up to go and Daisy walked out with him. She said, "Do you think it was the murderer? Was anything taken?"

"I don't know. It didn't look like anything was disturbed, but maybe you could come by in the morning and go through it with me."

"Of course. I just don't understand what this is all about."

"Me neither. Until we can figure it out, see if you can convince that old lady to stay somewhere else."

"I'll try, but I think it will be a waste of time. She's rather stubborn."

Brian looked at her and said, "I'm sorry our date was cut short." He leaned down and kissed her. Then he turned and walked off into the night. Daisy watched him go and said, "Me, too."

She walked back into the living room just as Angela was saying, "I'm staying with you, Adele, and that's that! The EMT may or may not have known what she was talking about, but you got a pretty nasty bump on the head and shouldn't be alone."

Adele slowly pushed herself out of her chair. "I'm too tired to argue, but you don't have your things."

Rose said, "Don't worry about Mother. She has everything she needs in that suitcase she calls a purse."

"You make it sound peculiar that I happen to keep clean undies, make-up, and a toothbrush with me. You never know when a situation just like this may arise. I, like any good Girl Scout, like to be prepared. Now get out of here and let us get some rest."

As they were driving home Rose asked, "Did Brian say they found anything at all?"

"No. He wants me to come back in the morning and go through the mansion with him, but he said nothing seemed to be disturbed." She smacked the steering wheel with her hand. "It's all so weird! Whoever this is doesn't take anything. Why would you kill Wally and assault Adele if all you were doing is wandering around the house? Sure, you'd be in a little trouble, but nothing like murder."

"I have no idea. Do you think Mother and Adele will be all right?"

"I think they'll be fine. In fact, I'm not sure this guy would be a match for the two of them together. And I've got a strange feeling about Amelia. I don't think she's a normal cat."

"No? What do you think it is, a large mouse in disguise?"

"I think it's a ghost-cat that Sophia sent to watch over Adele."

"Holy freaky felines, Daisy! It's just a stray! Get a grip."

They rode the rest of the way home in silence. But as soon as they got into the living room Daisy saw Rose's blond wig sitting on the table and said, "Rats! We didn't get to listen to Dad's conversation with Len Rutherford. I'd really like to know what those two are up to. And what they were doing after Dad left Mother's house. And where the heck was Leo tonight? And what's Mother going to do about that writing on her tree?"

"All good questions which will, no doubt, be answered in the morning." She looked at the clock over the fireplace. "Which, by the way, isn't too far off. I'm going to bed. We've got a lot to do tomorrow."

Saturday morning Daisy hung up the phone in the shop and said, "I'm going to go meet Brian at the mansion and do a walk-through. Then I'll pick Mother up. Should be back in an hour or so. Can you manage?"

Rose said, "Sure. Take your time. Tonya will be here soon and there's not much going on."

Two hours later Daisy, Rose, and Angela were sitting around the kitchen table sipping tea. "Well, did you and Brian find anything odd?" asked Rose.

"Not in the way you mean. On the other hand, it was very odd. Nothing was broken or out of place. We looked all around the basement, even in the storage area. Not a footprint. No paint. No scratches on the locks. If Adele hadn't been hurt, I'd have said it was a ghost."

"Well, it wasn't a ghost," said Angela. "Adele was very lucky she didn't break anything. She's a stubborn old thing and still refuses to leave, but she did promise not to go wandering around alone and to keep the alarm set even during the day."

"Did you get hold of Leo?"

"Yes. He finally answered his cell shortly before you got there, Daisy. He says he's out of town, a last minute business trip."

"You don't believe him?"

"How many high school teachers do you know that are suddenly called out of town? I think something fishy is going on."

"Could be. Or he could just be having a weekend fling with someone and not want his old auntie to know. Mother, what are you going to do about Dad?"

"I'm not entirely sure yet, but I don't think I'm going

to let on that I've seen the 'ghost' writing on the tree. I want to see just how far he's planning on going with this idiocy."

Rose said, "I do, too. But I also want to know where that paint came from. Dad couldn't be the mysterious marauder, could he?"

"With your father, a lot of things may be possible. But not murder. He wouldn't hurt anyone, not physically anyway."

Angela pulled out her phone. "Let's see what that Mr. Rutherford and Dickie were talking about last night."

The recording wasn't very good. Dickie was sitting closer to the phone and his voice was fairly clear, but Len Rutherford's was an indistinct mumble. It was like listening to someone on the phone, getting only one side of the conversation and guessing at the other. After some boring chit-chat about Maryland history, the Ravens chances this year, and, "My God, they make a mean Zombie in this place," Dickie said, "Just what do you think about this business up at the mansion?"

"Really? So you don't think it's the ghost breaking in?"

"Well, no, I suppose a ghost wouldn't need to whack someone on the head to kill him. I mean a ghost could just scare the man to death."

"Sure, I do. All old houses must have ghosts. Lots of people died in them. You know, thinking about it, I wonder if hospitals have a lot of trouble with ghosts. Think of how many poor suckers bite the dust in those joints. What do you think is going on if it's not ghosts?"

"Treasure hunters? I guess it could be. Have the police told you anything?"

"Oh, so you can reopen to the public? I guess that means Daisy will be back up there working. I have a favor to ask. I'd like your help with…" The rest of the sentence was cut off by the sound of a child throwing a fit in the booth across the aisle.

A minute later, they could hear Dickie again. "Thanks, Len. That might just work. Whoa, look at the time. Well, this has been great, but I've to get going. I've got a couple more stops to make before I can call it a day."

Then they could hear Len Rutherford say, "… swing by tonight… Keep an eye…"

After that it was just dishes clanking and mumbling in the background.

Angela said, "Well, that wasn't tremendously enlightening."

Rose played the recording again. "Not tremendously, no. But it raises a few questions. Just what kind of favor can Len Rutherford help him with? Exactly what is Dad up to with this sudden interest in ghostly goings-on and Holly Hill Mansion? And what other stops did he plan for that night? Did he have more trees to paint?"

Roscoe sauntered in from the kitchen and meowed loudly. Daisy brightened up a bit. "I think he's saying Ouija!" The cat jumped into her lap and meowed again. "He is. He thinks we should ask the Ouija board. He's very good at it."

"Who is?" Rose asked.

"Roscoe. Remember the last time we played Ouija and Dad was here pushing the pointer around – I know he insisted he wasn't, but we all know he was – and he spelled out 'reconcile'. Well, right after you threw him out, Mother, Roscoe put his little paws on the pointer and very clearly spelled out B.S. Now if that wasn't right on the money, I don't know what is."

She jumped up dumping the cat on the floor, grabbed the board and set it out on the table. "We should light a candle and do this right."

Angela got up and found a candle. Roscoe hopped up onto the table and purred. Rose just sighed in resignation.

"Okay, ladies. Who should we try to contact, Lydia or Sophia?"

Angela said, "I think we should ask Sophia who Adele is in danger from."

"Oh, yes we should," said Daisy. "Fingertips on the pointer please." Angela and Daisy touched the little triangle lightly. Rose said, "I think I'll just watch."

"Suit yourself. Now, let's clear our minds and think positive thoughts. Even you can think positive thoughts, Rose." Daisy closed her eyes and breathed deeply. "Ouija, are you there?"

The pointer didn't move. She tried again. "Ouija, are you there? We have an important question for Sophia Long."

"Maybe we're pressing too hard," said Angela. "Just a light touch. Try again."

"Ouija, can you contact Sophia? Is Adele Long in danger?" She waited. Still no movement. "What's wrong with this dumb thing? Why won't it answer?"

Rose answered, "Because it's a piece of plastic, not a spirit from the other side."

"Well, if that's your attitude, of course it won't answer," said Daisy. "Now be quiet while we concentrate."

They tried for the next five minutes with no hint of movement. Angela patted Roscoe on the head and said, "It was a nice idea, little buddy, but I guess the spirits aren't with us today. Sophia is probably worn out from the séance the other night."

As soon as the ladies left the room Roscoe put his paw on the pointer. It started moving across the board spelling out L-I-O-N, but nobody was there to see it.

Chapter Thirteen

Daisy was up early Sunday morning. She had brewed a pot of tea, fed the animals, and made cinnamon rolls which were sending a heavenly smell through the house as they baked.

As she stood looking out the kitchen window she breathed in the beautiful Indian summer day. She laughed at the squirrels who were putting on a daring acrobatic display in the tree tops. She smiled at one little guy who moved from spot to spot on the lawn digging holes. She looked around the familiar kitchen and beamed as the sun lit up the pale yellow of the walls. Finally, she picked up the morning paper and sighed contentedly as she sipped her tea.

Rose came into the room yawning. "You're up early. What smells so good? And what's with the silly grin? Let me guess – Brian Hathaway."

"I do not have a silly grin. I do happen to be feeling rather cheerful this morning. And, yes, it may have to do with Brian." Brian had come by the night before and he and Daisy had spent a cozy evening watching *Sense and Sensibility* and eating popcorn. "I think I could really like this guy. Not only does he love animals, especially rabbits, but he enjoys Jane Austin. He also thinks Mother is a fascinating woman, finds Malcolm's humping funny, brought a bottle of chilled Prosecco and insisted on making the popcorn himself. I think he may very well be the perfect man."

"Any word on the investigation?"

"That is one area where he's letting me down.

Except telling me that the mansion has been cleared to open and to please be careful because there is still a murderer on the loose, he wouldn't tell me a thing. I don't think he knows any more than we do."

"Actually, we might know a bit more than he does. Unless you told him about the séance and the lion falling over."

"Why Rose, I do believe you're becoming a 'believer'."

"Maybe I am. Not about the Ouija board. That's just silly. But something certainly happened at Adele's the other night. I've been thinking about it, trying to figure out how someone could have rigged the fog, the noises, the lion falling over. Let's just say I'm not as skeptical as I was. So, did you tell him about it?"

"No. He laughed when I mentioned the séance, so I didn't bother giving him the whole story."

The house phone rang. "What fool is calling at 8:30 on a Sunday morning?" Rose got up to answer it. "It's for you. Len Rutherford."

Daisy took the phone motioning for Rose to take the rolls out of the oven then went into the living room. A few minutes later Rose heard her slam down the phone.

"What did he want?"

Daisy picked up her tea and took a sip. Then she took a deep breath and counted to ten. "He was calling to let me know that Holly Hill is open for business and that he scheduled a bus tour for one o'clock. Unfortunately, he can't make it today. Something came up. I am on the roster with Joy Phillips, but she's sick. Alice Joseph has to stay in the Visitor Center. So it's all me. And, and by the way, he'd appreciate it if I could get there a little early." She sighed loudly. "I was having such a nice morning. I think he's going to be a bigger pain than Wally was. I don't suppose you'd like to come and help me, would you?"

Rose took a bite of her roll and said, "These are delicious. I'll come if you want me to, but I don't know enough to give a tour."

"You don't need to. Just help me keep an eye on them. You'd be amazed at the way some people behave. I've had parents let their kids run wild, even encourage them to put their grubby little hands on the very old objet d'art. I've had adults who sit on the furniture. I had one man who wanted to jump on the bed. I can deal with a small group, but a bus load needs at least two people, as any idiot must know."

"Okay, I'll do it. Peter's at a conference and I don't have anything planned."

The afternoon was worse than Daisy had predicted. She and Rose got to Holly Hill at twelve-thirty to be greeted by twenty-seven Japanese tourists who spoke no English and an American guide who didn't speak much Japanese.

Daisy thought to herself that if she could get her hands on Len Rutherford right that minute, Brian might be investigating another murder, this one a justifiable homicide.

The tour took well over two hours what with translating questions and answers, four separate trips to the restroom, and waiting for the slowpokes to catch up as they moved from room to room. Rose had brought up the rear and more or less herded the group while Daisy gave the lecture.

Finally, they were escorted to the door and Daisy motioned them down the path to the gift shop in the Visitor Center.

Rose was counting heads as they left. "I feel like a sheep dog. Uh oh."

"What?"

"I only counted twenty-six."

"What do you mean?"

"I mean that there were twenty-seven people and the guide when the tour started and now there are only twenty-six. We lost one."

"Oh my God." She ran after the guide and he gathered the group together outside the Visitor Center. Sure enough, they were missing Mr. Ito. Daisy sent them into the gift shop and went back to search for the missing tourist with Rose.

Rose had already checked upstairs. "Where could he be?"

Daisy called out, "Did you check the third floor?" The upper levels of the house weren't on the tour, but people were often curious.

"Yes. I went all the way up to the attic. Would he have gone into the basement?"

They walked to the cellar stairway. The door was closed. The police had taken the yellow tape down, but had posted NO ENTRY sign on it. "I guess we should look. I doubt Mr. Ito could read the sign."

They opened the door and went down the stairs. They stopped when they got to the bottom of the steps. Daisy called again, "I don't think he came this way." She turned the wall light on and looked around. "Mr. Ito, you're not down here in the basement, are you?"

They were turning to go back up when they heard a banging sound in the servants' hall. Daisy and Rose looked at each other. Daisy said, "Sophia?"

Rose said, "That's not a ghost. Listen. Someone's yelling. It sounds like angry Japanese."

They walked into the large servants' room and listened. Suddenly Daisy shouted, "The elevator!" and walked over to the bulletin board. "Here, help me move this. The door is behind it."

"There's an elevator? I didn't know that. Where does

it go?"

"To the dining room and the master bedchamber, but no one uses it. You need the key to open it from either side."

"Why?"

"I have no idea. It's just how it is."

"Well, that's just crazy."

Daisy knocked on the panel and said, "Mr. Ito?"

There was a lot of pounding and yelling on the other side. "Mr. Ito, we'll get you out. Just hold on."

Daisy took her keys out and shook her head. "I don't have it. I'll have to run over to the office."

Rose said, "What kind of idiot puts in an elevator that needs keys?"

"How should I know? Just stay here and keep him calm."

"Well, hurry." Rose knocked softly on the door. "Mr. Ito, don't worry. It will just be a minute while my sister gets the key. I'm Rose. You know, the lady who kept asking you all to stay together. But you didn't listen, did you? Of course, you can't understand a word I'm saying right now, can you? But I'm pretty sure you knew what I meant when I was waving all of you from room to room." She continued babbling until Daisy got back holding an old skeleton key and unlocked the door.

Mr. Ito came out huffing and puffing and ranting in Japanese.

"Well, if you'd stayed with the tour this wouldn't have happened, now would it?" Daisy took him by the arm and led him up the stairs, out the door, and to the gift shop. She handed him over to the guide with a sigh of relief. "All present and accounted for."

As she and Rose walked back to the house, Daisy said, "At least no one else came by for a tour. I don't know what I would have done. Lenny boy is getting an earful the next time I see him! Okay, we just need to make sure all is secure, that no one else is trapped anywhere, and we can turn out the lights and then we're out of here."

They worked their way from the attic down to the first floor. Everything seemed to be in good shape – no broken vases, missing salt cellars, and, most importantly, no additional mislaid Japanese businessmen trapped in closets.

When they got to the first floor Daisy said, "Rose, check the dining room, I'll get the parlor." Rose stood in the center of the beautiful room with its sixteen-foot ceiling, vivid green patterned wall paper, white marble mantle, mahogany furniture, and overstuffed sofa and looked all around. "This is a gorgeous room, but I don't see an elevator."

Daisy came in and closed the door. She pointed to a panel hidden in the design of the wall paper.

"The open dining room door hides it, but even when the door's closed, it's hard to spot."

Rose said, "How in the name of Elisha Otis did Mr. Ito find it?"

"More to the point, how did Mr. Ito get into it? And when?"

"I'll bet he wandered off before you ever got to the dining room. There's was a gap between your moving on to the next room and me waiting for the stragglers."

Rose examined the wall and asked, "How do you get this thing up from the basement?"

"The button there on the wall that looks like a light switch. But it just calls it up, it doesn't open the door."

"Then even if Mr. Ito was playing with the switch he couldn't have gotten in without the key. The door must have been open!"

"Well, I can't think why it would be. At any rate, I don't really care. I've had it for today. I'm going home, nursing a vodka tonic, ordering Chinese and getting lost in Downton Abbey."

"Sounds like a plan."

Monday evening as the final meeting of the Poe Night committee was breaking up Len took Daisy aside and said, "Could I have a word?"

"Just what I was thinking."

He put his arm around her shoulder. "I understand there was a problem yesterday. We really can't have visitors getting lost in the Hall. I thought I could count on you. You've let me down, Daisy."

Daisy moved away quickly. Then she opened her mouth to reply, but quickly shut it. She closed her eyes, took a few deep breaths, and silently started counting. She had gotten to thirty-three when Len said, "Well?"

"Well? Well, what kind of idiot schedules a bus tour without checking to make sure enough docents are available to handle it? You're just lucky my sister could help out or poor Mr. Ito might still be locked in the elevator."

He took a moment, then said, "You're right. I owe you an apology. I should have checked the schedule. It was very thoughtless of me. I can only blame it on the fact that I'm new to this position and that is no excuse. However, I don't understand why you had the elevator open."

"I didn't. I don't even have a key. Someone must have left it open."

"Well, that seems unlikely. I've spoken to everyone on staff and no one has used the elevator. Of course, the police were in here, too, but they don't have keys to anything."

"I was here Saturday with Detective Hathaway. He asked me to go through the house with him to see if anything was missing. I'm sure the elevator wasn't open. I'd have noticed that. However, the fact is that Mr. Ito got in somehow, so the door must have been ajar Sunday afternoon." She looked around the room and shivered. "I wonder if our resident burglar was here."

"I guess he could have been. That would explain a lot. I'm going to call the police and let them know about this."

"Good idea," said Daisy. "Well, then, good-night."

But Len stopped her. "I was wondering if I could take you out for a drink, an apology for my mishandling of the tour."

He looked so regretful that she didn't have the heart to turn him down.

"Well, it was odd. I couldn't tell if we were supposed to be on a date or what."

The next morning Daisy was telling Rose about her evening with Rutherford as they unpacked a shipment of stained glass window art. Rose said, "I'll bet he's got a crush on you."

"I'm afraid he might. He was way too touchy-feely. Kept patting my arm or my hand. And then, kiss of death in any relationship, he ordered for me without asking what I wanted."

"Maybe he's just old fashioned."

"He ordered me a lemonade. He had a dirty martini. Do I look like someone who wants lemonade?"

"Well, at least he wasn't trying to get you drunk."

"No. But when we left he planted a wet one right on my lips. Totally unexpected and more than a little creepy."

"What did you talk about?"

"Not much. He asked a lot of questions about us. I was regaling him with tales of Mother and her various oddities hoping he'd lose interest. That didn't faze him.

"But when I happened to mention how much I like our pets and that Malcolm and Percy are part of the family, he got really weird. You'd have thought I'd just told him that I had once been locked up for doing a Lizzie Borden, but they let me out on the promise that I'd stay on my meds and that, oops, I had forgotten to take them that morning. Apparently, he not only dislikes animals, he is terrified of dogs."

"A lot of people are."

"Well, I've never heard anyone get quite so petrified just hearing about them. Anyway, we got off that subject rather quickly and moved on to the problems at the mansion. We were trying to figure out why in the world the elevator was open and how our resident burglar is getting in and out of the place. The only explanation I could come up with is that he has keys."

"That would explain a lot. Could you price these and hang them in the sunroom?"

Daisy held up the panel. The rose and green glass glittered in the morning sun. "Sure. These are beautiful. I wonder how he got them?"

"I ordered them from a studio in North Carolina. How else would we get them?"

"Not the stained glass, the keys."

"Anyone can have a key made. And the elevator key is just an ordinary skeleton key. You should talk to Brian and see what he thinks."

"I did last night after I got home. And he thinks I should stay out of the investigation. What is it with policeman thinking they can tell me what to do?"

"I take it the bloom is off the rose."

"No, not really. He was sweet. We talked and I told him that you and I had been pretty helpful in the past catching bad guys. He said, 'And according to your ex, you almost got killed, didn't you?' and then suggested in the nicest way that we let him handle it."

"He talked to Bill?"

"Apparently. God knows what he told him. Why can't that man just leave me alone?"

"What man?" Angela Forrest practically flew into the shop waving a piece of paper in the air. "If you're talking about your father, he doesn't seem to be able to leave any of us alone. Look what I got in the mail this morning!"

She slammed the paper onto the counter and said, "Phony baloney, I am almost positive that imbecile wrote this himself."

It was a letter from Dickie's aunt Lydia dated the day before she died. In it she asked Angela to forgive Dickie his past indiscretions and to please consider taking him back. She went on to say that family was so important and the Dickie has lately come to realize how wrong he'd been and how much he had changed. Dickie thought that Lydia writing to her might help Angela understand how very remorseful he is and find it in her heart to forgive him.

"Well, that's interesting," said Daisy. "I don't believe a word of it, but it's interesting. Do you think he brainwashed her?"

Rose asked, "Is this Lydia's handwriting?"

"It could be. I don't have much to compare it with other than a line on a Christmas card," said Angela. "But why would she? I know that Lydia was furious with Dickie when he left us and I can't recall her ever saying she'd forgiven him. And at the funeral Marie was none too friendly to him. No. I think that fool sent this himself."

"Could he have forged the handwriting?"

Angela sniffed. "Well, he always fancied himself as something of an artist. Con artist, perhaps, and I think this proves it. At any rate, he's asked me out tonight and I've accepted."

"You've what?" Rose almost shouted.

"Mother," said Daisy, "why would you do that?"

"Because I want to know why he's doing all this." She turned away from them and stared out the window. "And because we were happy once. And, if you must know, deep down I want him to explain himself if he can. To take away some of the hurt."

Daisy and Rose were silent for a few moments. Then Daisy said, "Do you need a sidekick? I'm available."

"Me, too. Happy to hang out in the next booth dressed like a drag queen. I've got the wig already. Daisy can wear the bag lady dress. He won't know we're there."

Angela smiled. "No thank you. This is between Dickie and me. There is just a slim chance that Lydia really wrote that letter and that your father is a changed man. Of course, I'm not betting my Spanx on it. But whatever he's after, I believe it's my turn to call the shots."

Chapter Fourteen

"Stop pacing!" Daisy was walking back and forth across the living room followed closely by Malcolm and Percy. "You're making me crazy. And you're annoying Roscoe."

Roscoe was watching the little parade, tail twitching, ready to pounce, and making little chirping sounds.

Daisy said, "I can't help it, Rose. We should have gone with her. What if he tries to take advantage of her?"

"Oh for heaven's sake, what is Dad going to try? Mother's not an idiot. She's hardly going to give him money or lend him a credit card. And she's certainly not going to hop into the sack with him."

"That's not what I'm afraid of. I'm thinking he could break her heart again. How do you know she's not going to hop in the sack with him?"

"Did you see what she was wearing?" Angela had stopped by before her date. "I've never seen Mother look dowdy. She has looked insane on occasion, but never dowdy. However, tonight she looked just plain, well, plain. Brown sweater, high neckline, baggy slacks, no shape, no jewelry. I didn't think she owned anything like it. The message was clear, 'Don't even think it!'"

"I hope you're right." She started to pace again. "I need to do something. I can't just sit here all night."

"Evidently not. You're wearing the floor out."

Daisy stopped suddenly, causing a two dog pile-up.

"I know. We'll go up to Holly Hill and search the grounds. The dogs need a walk and it's a nice night."

"What would we be searching for?"

"I don't know - clues."

"You want to go up there and search the grounds for clues in the dark by ourselves with a murderer on the loose even after Brian asked you not to butt in?"

"Yes."

"Just so you don't have to worry about what our parents may be up to."

"Yes."

"And if we don't you're going to walk back and forth all night and sigh?"

"Pretty much."

Rose thought a minute. "Okay, we'll go."

It was a beautiful fall night. Clouds drifted lazily across the sky, occasionally obscuring the light of the moon. The air smelled of burning leaves and late blooming honeysuckle. Malcolm and Percy sat happily in the back seat, noses stuck out the four inches of open window, enjoying the night air.

"What's your plan?" asked Rose.

"I'd like to find how this guy is getting in."

"I thought you'd decided that the burglar has a key."

Daisy said, "Well, I think he has a key to the elevator. But that's just an old skeleton key. Anyone could have one. Antique shops sell them by the dozen. No, I think this guy is getting into the house some other way. The entrance locks are pretty sophisticated and he'd doesn't seem to know the alarm code."

"A clever criminal could have reset it to make you think he didn't know it or to make it look like no one got in."

"A really clever criminal would find another way in and wouldn't need to reset the alarm."

As they got near to Adele's Malcolm, and then Percy, let out a single mournful howl.

Rose patted their heads and said, "What's up, guys?"

"They remember our ghostly encounter with Sophia. This is where we saw her." Daisy turned to the dogs. "It's all right, no ghosts tonight."

They turned into the drive and slowed down as they passed Adele's house. Rose said, "It looks like all the lights are off. Adele must be asleep. Let's go on up to the Hall."

Daisy started to move forward when Rose said, "Wait a minute. I could swear I saw something moving near the house."

"Maybe we should check and make sure everything's okay."

Daisy pulled over and parked on the verge. They put the dogs on their leashes and walked up Adele's driveway, circled around the little white house, and came to the backyard gate.

Daisy said, "What do you think? Did you see something or not?"

"I'm not sure. Maybe we should take a quick look back here." The gate squeaked loudly as Rose pushed it open. The moon glowed brightly lighting up the lawn and the flower beds. "Looks quiet and the dogs aren't freaking out. Should we knock just to make sure she's all right. She might have heard the gate squeal."

They had barely gotten to the door when it opened. Adele was standing there in a gorgeous vintage purple silk and cream lace dressing gown, her hair in a long grey braid, reading glasses perched on her nose, and L. L. Bean Wicked Good moccasins on her feet. "I sensed it might be you."

"We would have knocked," said Daisy, "but we didn't see lights on and thought you might be asleep."

"No. Not asleep. I was in the sitting room reading when I heard the gate. It's really as good as an alarm."

"We didn't mean to disturb you. Adele, that's a simply stunning robe!"

"Thank you. It was my mother's, an original Mariano Fortuny." Adele stared at them over her glasses and asked, "What were you doing in my back garden?"

"Oh, Rose thought she saw something or someone moving."

"And just why are you here at this time of night, at all?"

"To keep Rose from going crazy."

She looked at Rose and asked, "And why were you going crazy?"

Rose sighed. "Mother and Dad are on a date of sorts. Daisy was so worried she couldn't keep still and it was driving me nuts. So, we decided to come to the mansion to search for clues. And then I thought I saw something moving near your house and we stopped to take a look."

"You probably saw a shadow. There are many of them lurking."

"A shadow? I guess it could have been a shadow," said Rose.

"At any rate, there was nothing there and you're clearly safe, so we'll just get out of your hair," said Daisy. "We're going to explore the Hall grounds, so if you see lights bobbing around, no need to call out the troops."

"That's fine. Be careful. Not all shadows are friendly. Oh, and the police have been coming by every hour or so. I saw the patrol car just ten minutes ago. You might want to leave your car here."

"Thanks. We won't be long."

As they were walking up the drive to the mansion

Daisy said, "Well, that was little odd, don't you think?"

"Yes, I do. She sounded almost, not exactly unfriendly, just sort of cold."

"Maybe she was asleep and didn't want to admit it."

"Maybe. But I got the feeling that she didn't want us there."

"Me, too. And what's with the 'shadows'. Does she mean ghosts or just shadows? I never noticed Adele being quite so strange when Aunt Lucille was alive."

"Probably because Aunt Lucille was a little peculiar herself. Now that I think of it, I'm fairly sure she might have dabbled in the occult, too. We were pretty small, but I seem to remember her laying out Tarot cards. Of course, I didn't realize what they were."

"Huh. Well, here we are." They stood in the dark staring up at the big empty house, hearing unseen creatures skittering about in the bushes. The wind picked up and clouds blocked the moonlight completely. Adele's wind chimes tinkled faintly in the breeze. An owl screeched and the dogs growled softly. Rose said, "Suddenly, this doesn't seem like such a good idea."

"Oh, come on. We've got the dogs and Adele knows we're here. And I brought a flashlight. Follow me." Daisy turned on the light and tugged at Malcolm's leash.

They walked around the Hall to the west, Rose and Percy trailing behind. They passed the carriage house which was locked up tight and skirted the walled garden at the rear. But as they got near the old kitchen both dogs started whimpering as a bank of fog rolled across the path in front of them. When it cleared she looked up to see a woman in a white gown with a string of pearls woven in her golden hair holding a basket standing at the edge of the trees. A moment later the fog rolled by again and she was gone.

Rose whispered, "Holy hallucinations!"

Daisy picked up Malcolm who was trying to climb her leg and said, "It's okay. It's only Sophia. We like her. Rose, she's trying to show us something. Come on."

"Daisy, I think you've lost your mind. It's time to go home."

"We can't go home. Sophia is showing us a clue. We can't let her down."

"This is too weird. I'm pretty sure ghosts and I do not mix well!"

"So you finally believe she's real! Come on, Sophia's a sweetheart. She'd never hurt anyone. Now if we had seen old Josiah I'd be running for the hills." She took off toward the rear of the kitchen and almost tripped over the wooden door to the cellar that was set perpendicular to the ground.

Rose caught up and said, "Daisy, don't you dare go off by yourself. If you insist on doing this, we can't get separated."

"I knew your curiosity would win."

"Not so much curiosity as you're the one with the light. The moon only works when it's not hidden by the clouds. What is that, a storm cellar?"

"It's the root cellar where they stored vegetables in the old days, but it can double as a storm cellar. I've only been in there once, years ago. This is where I found the map fragment. It was stuck in the hinge." Daisy examined the doors. "That's odd. This should be pad-locked." She pulled at the double door and it opened easily. "And someone's oiled the hinges. Hey, this is neat. We came looking for clues and we found one."

"I think Brian is right and we should leave this to him."

"Oh pshaw! We'll just take a quick look." She shone the beam down the little staircase leading to the cellar.

"No spider webs. I don't see any bugs. Let's go."

She was down the steps with Malcolm and Percy close on her heels leaving Rose standing alone in the dark. She looked around, took a deep breath, then followed her sister.

Daisy said, "It's bigger than I remember." The cellar was just high enough for Rose to stand up, but her head brushed the ceiling. The dirt floor sloped slightly. Shelves lined the walls.

Rose shivered. "It's cold in here. And damp." She looked around as Daisy explored the room with her flashlight. "And empty. Let's go."

"Wait a minute. Hold this." Daisy gave Rose Malcolm's leash and walked the perimeter of the room. She got to the wall nearest the mansion, stopped and bent down, then turned off her light.

"What are you doing? Turn that back on."

"In a minute. I saw something." They stood in the pitch dark and Daisy said, "Look!" A smear of grey paint glowed eerily next to Daisy's foot. She turned her light back on and studied the shelving. She shouted, "I knew it! Come here and help me move these shelves."

"Why?" Rose watched as Daisy took the top shelf down. "Oh my goodness! It's a door."

"Yep. Someone was using that paint as a marker."

They got the shelves down and uncovered what looked like a small door set into the wall. But there was no handle. Rose said, "How do you open it?"

"How do I know? Maybe we'll need a crowbar."

Rose examined the door. "I don't think so. I don't see any marks on it. There must be some other way."

Daisy ran her hands over the wall. "Maybe it only opens from the other side."

The dogs had been sitting patiently watching them. Malcolm got up and trotted around the room, sniffing and snuffling. He stopped and sat on the floor right under the paint smear. They heard a crack and the door began to open slowly.

Daisy bent down and ruffled his head. "What a clever boy you are! Come on." She bent down and charged through the door.

Rose cried, "For heaven's sake, wait a minute. Let's think this through. You don't know where this leads, if it leads anywhere. You could be walking into some sort of trap. And you have no idea whether you can get out of there once you're in if this door closes."

Daisy hesitated and came back out. "You're right. Okay, let's do this. You close the door and I'll see if I can open it from the other side. Give me a couple of minutes. If I don't come out, you can open it for me."

Rose sighed, "This is so dumb. I should just leave you in there. Besides, it's dark in here and you have the light."

"Where's your phone?"

"I left it in the car. I didn't know we'd be breaking into cellars and tunnels."

"We didn't break in. Here." She took out her cell phone and turned on the flashlight and handed it to Rose. "Happy now?"

"Not particularly," but she pushed the door closed shutting Daisy in the dark tunnel. Malcolm and Percy started to dig under it. Rose said, "Stop that. It's okay, guys. I'll let her out in a minute." They waited. She called to Daisy, but couldn't hear anything through the wall. After almost three minutes she was just getting ready step on the floor switch when the door popped open. "What took you so long?"

"I was looking for a hidden panel or something like the one on this side. But I just needed to push hard. This is so exciting. I cannot believe we actually found a tunnel. Let's see where it leads."

"Well, I think this is nuts, but I won't let you go in

there alone. However, I'm not taking the dogs. There's no reason they should die an untimely death locked in an airless tunnel just to please you."

"It's not airless and nobody is going to die." Daisy thought a moment. "But as long as we're being careful I think I'll just leave a little note with Malcolm mentioning where we are." She took a small pad out of her shoulder bag, wrote quickly and wrapped it around Malcolm's collar. "There. If we do get locked in somehow, Malcolm can go for help, can't you baby?" She gave him a little kiss on his head.

"Couldn't we just call for help?"

"Probably. This is just in case we can't get a signal in the tunnel."

Rose wrapped the dogs' leashes around one of the shelves. "You two stay here and keep watch. Bark like little mad puppies if anyone comes in." Then she wedged another shelf in the doorway. She murmured, "Just to be on the safe side. That phrase just took on a whole new meaning!"

The tunnel was a little over five feet high and four feet wide. Rose said, "My back is going to be killing me tomorrow. Daisy, do you have any idea where this goes?"

"Well, if it follows the dots on the map, I think we should be able to get to the basement of the mansion."

They moved forward for what seemed to Rose about a day and a half, but was actually only a few minutes. Then the tunnel took a sharp right hand turn. Daisy said, "This can't be right. The mansion should be straight ahead."

"Maybe there's another hidden door."

Daisy shone her light over the wall. "I don't see anything. We could have missed it in the passage. I wasn't looking at the walls."

"We can check on the way back." Rose sighed,

"We've come this far. We might as well keep going."

They walked on for what seemed like another day or so and finally came to wall blocking the passage.

Rose said, "What now?"

"I don't know. I can hardly see anything." Daisy's flashlight which had been getting dim went out. "Oops."

"Oops is right. Didn't you change the batteries?"

"I meant to."

Rose rolled her eyes to no effect since Daisy couldn't see her. "Let's go back before your cell phone gives out too. I do not want to be stuck in here in total darkness."

"Me neither. But first real fast, just shine it over the wall here. There must be a way through. No one would build a tunnel to go nowhere."

The beam was getting dimmer by the second. "I guess you meant to charge this, too, didn't you? We'd better hurry." But she shone the light over the wall and sure enough there was a door. This one had a lock.

Daisy said, "Well, isn't that just the cherry on top! We need a key."

"And we don't have one and we're not going to be able to see a damned thing if this light goes out."

Daisy turned reluctantly. "It wouldn't really matter anyway. We could hardly get lost in here."

"True. But I'm not fond of the thought of little creepy crawlies falling in my hair."

With Rose in the lead they were almost back to the cellar when the cell phone died. She stumbled and fell forward, barely catching herself, her hand landing on something cool and silky. Thinking she must have dropped her scarf, she picked it up and stuck it in her jacket pocket.

"Are you all right?" asked Daisy.

"Yes. Just be careful. The floor's not very even." They fumbled their way into the cellar and pushed the door closed. The moon was shining brightly again and cast just enough light through the outside door so they could manage to get the shelves back in place.

As they emerged from the cellar Rose took a deep breath of the evening air and said, "Well."

"Well what?"

"Just well. A ghost, a secret passage. I need a drink."

"Me, too. What time is it?"

"Almost eleven."

"Time to see if Mother has made it back unscathed."

Chapter Fifteen

"Are you going to tell Brian?" Rose asked as she poured tequila, orange juice and grenadine into two chilled glasses. Malcolm looked at her hopefully, but she just patted his head and said, "No way, buster. Tequila is not good for little dogs. Remember how sick you were last time? Here, have a biscuit."

Daisy sat on the couch fooling with her phone. "I don't want a biscuit, but the tequila sounds good."

Rose handed Daisy a glass and said, "Well, are you?"

"Am I what?"

"Going to tell Brian about our evening."

"What's to tell? We didn't find anything and he might get a little upset that we were looking. Besides, he does not need to know my every movement." She swirled the liquid in her glass. "Mother hasn't called yet."

"She's probably asleep already. I think you should tell him."

"She wouldn't go to bed without calling. She knows we're worried. Why should I tell him? The police had every opportunity to find that tunnel and they didn't. I even told Brian about the paint. If they didn't have enough sense to look thoroughly, well, tough beans."

Daisy's phone beeped. "It's Mother. She's texting." She opened the message and sighed. "I cannot believe she types this badly. I think she does it on purpose."

"What does it say?"

"Helo fiells. Im nome. All ylj in tne mor?inf."

Rose said, "Oh that's easy. Hello girls. I'm home. Call you in the morning."

"How do you do that?"

"It's a gift."

Daisy put the phone down and took a sip of her drink. "Why didn't she call? You don't think he's still with her, do you? I mean *with* her."

"That is something I don't want to know – ever. We'll just have to wait for the bright new day to find out what happened. Speaking of which, I'm going to bed."

"I'm right behind you."

Daisy couldn't sleep. She tossed and turned for a while, then turned on the light and pulled out an old Agatha Christie she'd read about twelve times. This usually worked on the rare nights when sleep was elusive. But not tonight.

After an hour she gave up on Agatha to try counting sheep. She turned off the light, closed her eyes and pictured little white bundles of fleece leaping over a split rail fence in the middle of a meadow. But when the three hundred and thirty-seventh little fur ball missed his aim and smacked his face right into the fence and fell on his little sheep butt, she gave up. Opening her eyes, she slipped out of bed, put on her sock-monkey slippers and old flannel robe, and tiptoed downstairs.

Houses in the middle of the night can be strange and unnerving. Everything seems quieter and louder at the same time. In the silence the clock over the mantel sounded like a time bomb ticking down the minutes to the big boom. A loose shutter was banging raucously in the wind. Ice cubes rumbled into the bin in the freezer and made Daisy start. Every creak of the old house was magnified. Daisy shivered, turned on the desk lamp, and said to the empty room, "Okay, I'll just have something hot to drink and get back to bed."

When Roscoe silently brushed her leg she screamed and jumped about three feet in the air. "Roscoe! You scared the hell out of me."

She went to the kitchen and put the water on for tea. Roscoe followed and jumped up onto one of the chairs. "Don't do that again, okay? Want some milk?" She poured a little bowl of milk for the cat and made herself a cup of Sleepy Time and they sat in companionable silence sipping and lapping. When Roscoe had finished, he leapt from his chair and jumped across the table into her lap. But as he leapt he managed to send his bowl flying across the room where it crashed into the bag of recycling ready to go out in the morning. Cans and bottles clattered out of the bag making an unholy racket.

As Daisy was re-bagging the mess she stopped suddenly and held her breath. Someone was sneaking across the living room. She picked up an empty wine bottle, a nice Gewurztraminer, by its long neck and stealthily moved across the kitchen, hugging the wall, until she came to the doorway. Taking a deep breath, she jumped into the living room, wine bottle raised in her right hand and shouted, "The police are on their way!"

"Daisy, what in the name of Froot Loops are you doing down here?" Rose shouted at the same time. She was standing in the middle of the room, baseball bat held high ready to whack something. "You scared me half to death."

"I scared you? Hells bells, I thought a burglar was sneaking around."

"I had the same thought, only my burglar was a tad noisy. Why were you making all that racket?"

"I couldn't sleep."

"So you thought playing Jenga with the wine bottles would help?"

"That was Roscoe. You know, we seem to have an inordinate number of wine bottles for just the two of us. I don't remember drinking that much this week, although if I actually drank that much I guess I wouldn't remember, would I?"

"You didn't. Neither did I. I've been saving bottles to make a craft thingy. But when I was putting the groceries in the pantry yesterday I realized that half the cupboard was filled with empty wine bottles. I had to admit to myself that crafty thing was never going to happen, so I threw them out."

"Ah, that explains it. Crafts can certainly be a burden. I was having a cup of tea, want one?"

"Tea sounds good. My heart is still racing. Are there any cookies left?"

As Rose nibbled a molasses cookie, Daisy sipped her tea and said, "This whole thing is making me nuts. That's why I couldn't sleep."

"I know. Tonight was really pretty spooky. And I now officially believe in at least one ghost."

But Daisy shook her head. "Sophia isn't what's getting to me. It's all the other stuff. If I were just seeing ghosts, well, that would be kind of fun. But it's such a big mess with Dad and Adele and Wally and tunnels and lions. I just can't figure out how any of this makes sense." She grabbed a cookie and chewed thoughtfully. "I do believe it's pad and pencil time."

"You know we have to get up in about four hours, don't you?"

"I know. But I'm wide awake and I know I'm not getting any sleep unless I make some sort of sense of this."

"All right, but you may need to cover for me while I take a nap this afternoon. Let's take a look at what we know from the beginning."

Rose got a pad of paper from the desk and wrote

across MANSION MURDER. "Okey dokey, let's start with the beginning. 1. Someone is getting into the mansion."

Daisy said, "No. that's not the beginning. I think we have to start way back when with Sophia and Josiah and the silver."

"Oh lord, this will take all night."

"No it won't. Give me the pad. I'll make a list and you can add anything I forget."

1.   We think Sophia hid her Revere silver somewhere on the grounds of Holly Hill. It hasn't been seen since.

2.   Sophia appeared to me and seemed to be telling me to do something. What?

3.   Dad shows up shortly after Aunt Lydia's funeral apparently trying to get Mother back. Why?

4.   Wally sets a trap for the burglar and gets snuffed out. Was it an accident or intentional?

5.   Who has been searching for the silver? Who is Howard Carter? Is that his real name?

6.   Who was in the mansion when Adele was attacked? Was it the same burglar or someone else? Where was Leo? Where was Len Rutherford? Where was Dad?

7.   Where did the scrap of map come from and how did it get wedged in the cellar door?

8.   Does Adele know about the tunnel and where does the tunnel we found lead - to the mansion or someplace else?

She handed the list to Rose and said, "What do you think?"

She looked it over and said, "Not bad. But we need to add a couple of things. First, we know Adele has at least one piece of the Revere silver. So, we need 1a - does Adele know where the silver is?"

"Good thinking."

"Also, number 9 - the séance. What the heck does 'lion' mean? It must mean something."

"Aha! I knew you were a believer at heart!"

"Whatever. 10 - Dad knows Len Rutherford. What's with that?"

"Oh yes. What is with that? Are they in this together? Should we add 11 - Could our father actually kill someone?"

"I really can't believe that. Let's make 11 – Could our father be in cahoots with a murderer? And that leads us to 12 – that paint on your dress, in the root cellar and the basement of the mansion. Who put it there?"

"And who cleaned it off before the police searched the place?"

"Indeed. And did it mark an entrance to the tunnel from the basement of the mansion? And did our father have anything to do with that or was his using the same paint just a coincidence? In other words, just what the heck is he up to?"

"Yes. That really is the biggest question. And is he up to it with Mother?"

Rose said, "I repeat, I don't want to go there." Roscoe jumped into her lap and purred contentedly as she scratched his ears and studied the list. "What do you think?"

"I think we need to get into the basement and see if we can find the entrance to the tunnel."

"I knew you'd say that. I think we should get some more history of the Long family and try to find out if there ever was a hidden treasure, who might know about the treasure and the tunnel, and how they might know it. And why, after all these years, is someone looking for it now. We have to talk to Adele!"

Daisy threw her pillow over her head as the alarm

screeched for the fifth time beside her bed. She reached a hand out to give it a smack, but it stopped abruptly before she got the chance.

"Rise and shine, darling," Angela Forrest cooed as she drew back the curtains letting the warm October sunshine into the room.

"Mother?"

"Time to get up. Breakfast is almost ready and Rose is getting dressed."

The aroma of something delicious wafted up from the kitchen. Daisy stretched and checked the clock – 8:45. "Holy smoke. I've got to move it. What do I smell?"

"Coffee cake. Tea's made."

Daisy sat up and rubbed her eyes. Then she got a good look at her mother. "Mother, why are you dressed like a Munich barmaid?"

Angela Forrest, dressed in a sapphire blue dirndl with a white blouse and apron, was combing through Daisy's closet. "Your father's taking us out for the day."

"To Germany?"

"Don't be silly. We're going to have a grand time. You haven't got a dirndl?"

"Why would I? Why do you? Besides, we can't go anywhere. We have a shop to run."

"That's all taken care of. Dot's going to help Tonya out so we can spend the day as a happy family. You always say Fridays are slow anyway."

"Mother, what's this all about? Oh, my God, you and Dad didn't do something really stupid last night, did you?"

Rose came into the room wearing black slacks and a sage green sweater. She said, "Yes. Did you do something stupid?"

"Well, if you consider bowling stupid, then yes we did."

Daisy hopped out of bed. "He took you bowling?"

Rose said, "You can bowl?"

"Of course. I bowled a decent four-seventy-five three-game series and beat your father quite handily! He was as mad as a wet hen. Actually, I've never seen a wet hen, so I'm not sure just how angry they get, but he was pretty annoyed."

"How about that. When did you start bowling?" Rose asked.

"Rose, who cares? What I want to know is what the heck sort of date is bowling? And what has any of this to do with dirndls?"

Angela handed Daisy a sage green jumper and black turtleneck. "This should do. You'll match Rose. Hurry up and I'll explain all while we eat."

Half an hour later they were sitting at the kitchen table eating coffee cake. Daisy moodily sipped her tea and said, "We look ridiculous. I feel like picture day in grade school. You always made us wear matching dresses." She put her cup down and tried to look her mother in the eye. "Okay, what's going on?"

But Angela was reading the list Daisy and Rose had made the night before. "This is good. It clarifies, doesn't it? But I don't think you'll get any answers out of Adele. I've already tried and she's not talking."

"We'll get to that in a minute," said Rose. "Why are Daisy and I skipping work today?"

"Because your father is taking us to an Oktoberfest celebration at a brewery downtown and then we are going to dinner. Afterward we'll be taking the Capitol Hill ghost tour. And we are doing this because I still have no idea what he's up to."

"Well, other than beating him soundly, how did the rest of the night go?"

"Fine. He was a perfect gentleman which, of course, made me more suspicious than ever. He just keeps saying that as he nears the end of his life he's reflecting on decisions he's made and trying to make amends. That family means everything to him and it just took him this long to realize it. You'd think he was in his late nineties and on death row."

"Well, maybe he has had an awakening," said Rose. "Or, I know he said he's fine, but maybe he's ill."

"Ill, my foot," said Angela. "No. He's not sick and he hasn't awoken to anything. And I don't trust him as far as I could toss an obese wombat. Our mission for today is to get the truth out of him."

At eleven that evening Daisy and Rose were sitting in their living room with Angela sipping hot toddies.

Daisy said, "Well, we learned nothing at all. I still have no idea why our father suddenly showed up put of the blue and wants to play happy families."

Rose thought a moment. "I wouldn't say we didn't learn anything. I now know that I don't particularly like IPAs, that I can't tell an American from an English or an Imperial IPA. And that if I hear one more person wax poetic about the hoppiness, herbalness, fruitiness, or earthiness of some damned beer they will get said beer dumped right over their hoppy little heads."

Angela petted Roscoe who was curled up in her lap. "And, of course, we learned all about the Demon Black Cat that haunts the Capitol building before disasters and Presidential inaugurations. Also, I myself would love to see Wilbur Mills running around. And that Judge Holt who haunts First Street sounds like he needs a friend."

"Okay, aside from discovering that we don't care for IPAs which isn't a surprise because none of us ever has liked beer except a Miller Lite with crabs in the summer and that apparently there are more dead congressmen on Capitol Hill than there are live ones, we still do not know why Dickie Forrest has returned," said Daisy,

Angela stretched. "And I have pretty much decided to forget about him for the present. I suppose he'll get to the point sometime."

"Mother, is Dad getting to you? I mean, you don't seem to be mad at him. And you were plenty angry when he showed up with his Ouija board in hand."

"No. It just seems that, without realizing it, I've forgiven him. I certainly don't want him back, but I don't want him deceased either anymore. Now I'm just curious. Meanwhile," she picked up the Mansion Murder list, "I think you two have made a good start here. However, as I said, I have tried to get information out of Adele, but all I got in answer was a sly smile and a cup of bourbon-laced tea."

Rose said, "I'm going to do some research on-line and see what I can come up with. There must be some record of a treasure like the Revere silver. And I'd like to know more about the family. Mother, Adele was putting out some weird vibes last night. Sort of like she didn't trust us."

"I can't imagine why she wouldn't, but she was acting quite odd when I spent the night with her. Maybe it's just her age catching up. Or, perhaps, Sophia and she have some sort of plan to catch Wally's killer. And it doesn't include us."

Rose raised her teacup and asked, "Anyone for another?"

Daisy nodded. "Sure."

"Mother? You are spending the night, aren't you?"

"Yes, dear. And yes to the toddy. It's been a long, long day."

Daisy got up and took the little piece of map from the desk. "I wonder what this came from."

Angela looked at it. "Well, I'm sure the paper is old,

maybe very old. It looks as if it were torn from some sort of book."

"That's what I was thinking."

Angela said, "I think you had better show me where you found it. And…"

"Here it comes. I can't believe you waited this long to bring it up." Rose handed them each a warm cup.

"Bring what up?"

"You want to search the mansion basement for a way into the tunnel."

Angela laughed. "Well, of course I do. Don't you?"

"Not really. This is something we should tell Brian about."

"And if we find something, we will," said Daisy. "We can't do it tomorrow. It's our Gothic Evening with Poe Night. Too many people will be around and I have to work."

"And I have a date with Peter. And Mother, remember that you promised Dad you would go paint pottery with him."

"I did, didn't I? That's what comes of one too many India Pale Ales."

Daisy shook her head. "Then how about Sunday evening after tours have finished?"

Angela nodded. "Sunday it is."

Rose just sighed and finished off her toddy.

Chapter Sixteen

The mansion was at its beautiful best Saturday evening. Candles lit each room and garlands of berries and vines hung over doorways and on mantels. A harpist played haunting melodies in the east wing while Mr. Poe, sounding an awful lot like Vincent Price, sat next to the fireplace in the parlor and read from his various works.

The Tavern in a Tent outside offered tankards of ale, glasses of wine and sparkling cider at the bar on one side of the room. An array of savory dishes and sweets was set out at a buffet on the other. Three fiddlers were playing lilting tavern tunes. The evening was sold out, as usual.

Only the first floor of the mansion was open to visitors and was staffed with a docent in each room. Len Rutherford floated about making sure no one snuck up stairs or into the basement. Adele, with Leo at her side, was in her glory greeting guests at the door. Dressed in a scarlet silk gown with an immense hoop skirt, her hair parted severely down the middle and pulled to a bun at the nape of her neck, she was truly a southern grand-dame. Her nephew, Leo, outfitted in matching gentleman's clothes, was her escort for the evening.

Daisy, declining to dress in period costume, wore an elegant black jersey tea length gown. She had custody of the dining room and spent the night repeating her talk about the family, entertaining in the early and mid-

1800s, and the furniture.

As she was describing to a nice young couple what an average dinner might consist of, she spotted Rose and Peter talking to Sally Henderson who was on duty in the parlor.

When they got to the dining room she said, "I didn't know you were coming."

Rose said, "I didn't either. Peter surprised me. You outdid yourselves this year. Everything is absolutely beautiful."

"So where exactly did you see the ghost?" asked Peter.

"Which time?"

"There was more than once?"

"Oh, yes. We both saw her the other night. Rose didn't mention it?"

Rose frowned at her sister and said, "I'll tell you all about it later. Let's go listen to Mr. Poe. He's reading *The Raven*." She took his arm and was about to lead him away when Angela, dressed in a pale blue smock and matching beret, and Dickie blew into the room.

Dickie boomed, "Well, the gang's all here! This is just great."

"Dad, could you not shout?" asked Daisy. "What are you doing here? I thought you were painting pottery."

Angela touched her beret. "Obviously, so did I."

Dickie grinned. "We can paint pottery anytime. When I heard about this shindig I said to myself 'Dick, that's where you have to be. How often do I get to hang out with all my girls?'"

"Dad, we haven't been girls for a while now and we haven't been *your* girls for longer than that."

Another couple came into the room and Daisy said, "You have to move. Go get a drink or listen to Mr. Poe. I've got work to do." Rose and Peter headed in the direction of the parlor, but Dickie said, "I want to hear your spiel." He and Angela stayed and listened to Daisy discuss dining in the early nineteenth century. "That was very interesting, honey. You make it come to life."

"Thanks, Dad. Now maybe you should move along. Lots more people want to see the room."

Daisy spent the rest of the evening giving her talk, preventing a couple who had had one too many tankards of ale from walking out with a Sevres custard cup, and wiping up wine spills.

By closing time at eleven o'clock she'd had it. Rose stopped on her way out and told her she and Peter were leaving, but they were picking up pizza. "Lord, you must be exhausted."

"I am. And I'd really like to get out of these damned shoes. Thank God the caterers clean up the tent. But I have to wait until everyone else is out of the house to lock up."

"I thought that was Len Rutherford's job."

"He asked if I could do it. He wasn't feeling well and left a while ago. I should be home in an hour or so. Could you save me a slice?"

"Sure. We'll keep it hot for you."

After seeing Mr. Poe, the harpist, a stray guest, and the last docent out Daisy went back to the dining room to retrieve her purse which she, like a lot of the docents, hid under the sofa when she was on duty. She pulled it out, then she decided to take a minute to sit down and rub her feet before she left. She dropped onto the sofa and felt something lodged under the cushion. She lifted the cushion expecting to find a wallet or small purse. What she found was a very old, leather bound book. She was standing with her back to the room slowly turning the pages when she felt her head explode and everything went black.

When Daisy came to everything was still black

except for the fireworks that seemed to be going off in her head. She was lying on a cold tiled floor, her head propped on a pillow. After a few minutes, she sat up, then tried to stand, but a wave of nausea caused her to lie back down. Closing her eyes, Daisy drifted off to sleep once again.

When she woke the next time, the fireworks had been replaced with a bass drum beating a steady rhythm. She sat there trying to get her bearings. "Where am I?" Her thoughts were fuzzy. She felt like she was trying to put a puzzle together, only all the pieces were grey. Struggling to remember what had happened, she reached out in the darkness and found that she could easily touch the four walls around her. "Am I in the elevator? Why am I in the elevator? And what's wrong with my head?" Her fingers touched the top of her head and felt something sticky matting her hair and a huge lump.

Tears sprang into her eyes, but she sniffed and took a deep breath. "Someone hit me." She tried to stand again, but the pounding got worse so she plopped back down. "I will not cry. I will not. I wonder if I have a concussion. I've never had one." She sniffed again. "I need a tissue and I should let Rose know I'll be late."

Her brain seemed to clear suddenly and she almost shouted, "My phone!" She searched the floor around her and her hand fell on her purse. She quickly rummaged through it, but couldn't find her cell. She shook the little bag and dumped the contents onto her skirt. The phone was definitely not there. She did find a tissue and an old granola bar which she opened and moodily nibbled while she tried to figure out if there was enough air in the elevator to keep her alive until someone found her. Then she cradled her aching head in her arms, and waited.

At two o'clock Rose nudged Peter awake and said, "How can you sleep? She still isn't answering. What should we do?"

Peter sat up and said, "Sorry. I didn't realize I'd nodded off. I think you should call Brian."

"She'll kill me if I get him involved and she's just snooping around the house or something."

"At two in the morning? Without telling you? The house was dark. If she's still there, she isn't snooping." At one o'clock Rose and Peter had driven back to the mansion to find it locked up tight. Rose even checked the kitchen root cellar only to find that the padlock was securely in place.

Suddenly Rose had a vivid picture of Wally Stone lying in the basement with his head bashed in. "You're right. I'm calling him. She can just be mad at me."

Brian Hathaway got to The Elms fifteen minutes later. Rose said, "That was fast."

"I was already in the area. Now, what's this about Daisy being missing?"

Rose told him about the evening and that they expected Daisy by midnight at the latest. "She's not answering her phone."

"Was her car there?"

"No. It wasn't."

"Could she be with your mother or her friend Marc?"

"She'd have called me. Besides she was so tired and her feet were killing her, she just wanted to come home and put her slippers on."

"Do you have a key to the mansion?"

"I don't, but Adele does."

Brian took his phone out and said, "We've still got a cruiser checking the place out every hour or so. Let me talk to them and see if they noticed anything." He stepped into the kitchen to make his call.

Rose paced while she waited. Brian came back and

said, "They're actually at the mansion now and her car is in the Visitor Center's lot."

"Well, it wasn't there an hour ago!"

Brian said, "I'm going over there. I'll have to wake up Ms. Long and get the key."

Rose picked up her jacket. "I'm going with you. Peter, you stay here in case Daisy comes home or calls the land line." They had just gotten to the front door when Rose said, "Just a sec," and ran back upstairs. She came back a moment later and said, "All set. Let go."

Rose called Adele from the car and she was on her porch waiting for them, key in hand. "And this is the alarm code. Should I come with you?"

Brian said, "No, ma'am. In fact, Rose, I think you should stay here with Ms. Long."

"Not going to happen. I couldn't just wait here. Besides two of us searching will be quicker."

They walked around the grounds, checked the kitchen and the coach house. Both were locked and dark. The padlock was still in place on the cellar door. Rose called out to Daisy over and over, but an occasional hoot from some unseen owl was the only answer.

Finally, Brian unlocked the side door of the mansion. They walked into the hall lit only by the amber glow from the alarm pad. Brian punched in the code. The house was silent and dark. Turning lights on as they moved from room to room they made their way along the hallway of the first floor calling Daisy.

When they got to the main staircase and Rose said, "You go down and I'll go up."

"No. We stick together. One missing Forrest sister is enough."

Rose wouldn't admit it, but she was relieved. The thought of roaming around the big dark house replete with ghosts and, possibly, a murderer wasn't particularly inviting. "Okay, where do we start?"

"What was Daisy meant to do here tonight?"

"She was stationed in the dining room. But then she had to lock up. Len Rutherford was supposed to do it, but he was sick and left early."

"Let's look at the dining room." They turned the lamp on in the corner. Everything looked in place. They moved through the rest of the rooms on the first floor. Nothing unusual. No dead bodies or bloody candlesticks were lying around.

"We'll work our way down from the attic," Brian said and they made their way up the steep winding servants' staircase and checked every room.

The attic and the second floor were empty. No closets or hiding places, although Rose did look under the beautiful four-poster in the master bedchamber and breathed a sigh of relief when all she saw were a lot of dust bunnies. "I guess we go to the cellar next."

The cellar was cold and dark and empty. No eerie glow-in-the-dark paint was visible. No Sophia lighting the way. Rose called Daisy's name and it echoed back at her. "What do we do now?"

"Search the grounds."

"That's eight acres, a lot of it woods. We can't do all that alone."

"Well, we'll start and as soon as it's light I'll call for reinforcements to help."

On their way out Rose stopped suddenly and said, "We didn't check the elevator!"

"The elevator?"

"Daisy told you about Mr. Ito getting stuck in the elevator, didn't she?"

They walked into the dining room and shut the door behind them. The door to the elevator was shut tight. But Brian shone his flashlight around that side of the room and saw something on the carpet that he hadn't noticed the first time they checked.

"Look at the carpet. I think something's been dragged across here."

Rose started banging on the door of the elevator. After a minute she thought she heard a faint tapping in response. She yelled, "Daisy, are you in there?"

Brian said, "How the hell do you get into this thing?"

Rose smacked her head and said, "With a skeleton key." She pulled out a ring with old keys on it. "I'm really losing it. I grabbed them before I left. I thought we might need them."

Brian took the keys and tried one after another until, finally, the lock turned. He opened the door. Daisy looked up and whispered, "It's about time," then fell heavily onto his feet.

Chapter Seventeen

A voice was saying, "Daisy, wake up." It was annoying, like a strand of hair caught in an eyelash. She couldn't swat it away. Her head was still pounding, but now she could sense light around her. She kept her eyes closed. She just wanted to go back to sleep, but the voice kept calling her. Daisy mumbled, "Go away," and drifted off into a bizarre dream.

She was lying under a couch paging through on old book in the dark. The spidery writing glowed on the pages in an eerie green light. She came to a page with a picture on it - a three ring circus. A line of clowns carrying shovels was moving in and out of the rings through little slits all around the sides of the tent. Then she saw Sophia standing beside a younger woman holding a little book. The woman had Sophia's deep blue eyes and slender neck, but her hair was dark, almost black. They were in the woods outside the tent. The young woman was crying, "I want to come home, but I've lost my way." Sophia smiled and held her arms out. "Of course, my darling girl. Come home. Come to me. Come…"

"Come on, Daisy. Time to wake up!"

Daisy opened her eyes to see Rose bending over her shining a flashlight in her face. "Point that somewhere else, would you?"

"Sorry. Do you know who I am?"

"What?"

"Do – you – know – who – I – am?"

"An irritating robot? Of course, I know who you are."

"Well?"

"Really? I have a splitting headache and you want me to tell you who you are?"

"Yes. I do."

"You're my idiot sister, Rose Forrest."

"Good. Good. Now do you know your name?"

"Oh for crying out loud, Rose. Is this what you learned in your first-aid course? How to annoy the victim?"

Daisy could hear a voice talking in the hallway. "Yes. And I need that ambulance up here now."

She sat up and leaned against the wall. "Is that Brian? We don't need an ambulance. I'm fine. Some aspirin and an ice pack and I'm good to go."

"Daisy, you are not good to go. You've been unconscious and you've got a knot on your head as big as an orange. You need a doctor."

Before Daisy could answer they heard a door slam and hurried footsteps. Angela flew into the room, hugged Daisy fiercely, looked into her eyes, and felt her forehead. "You seem to be all right."

Daisy glared at Rose. "You called Mother?"

"Of course not. You know she has that weird ESP thing."

Angela held up three fingers and asked, "How many fingers do you see?"

Daisy sighed. "For pity sake. Three! I see three fingers."

"Good. By the way, I do not have ESP. Adele called me, of course. Here, sweetheart, put this on your head." Angela opened her bag, took out an Instant Ice Pack, cracked it and handed it to Daisy.

Daisy took it and held it gingerly on her head. "Ouch!" She repositioned it and sighed. "How did you know I'd need an ice pack?"

"It was a safe bet. You and Rose seem to get hit on the head with alarming regularity."

"You don't happen to have some aspirin in that pharmacy you tote around, do you?"

"Yes, but we had better wait until the EMTs get here and check you out. I don't think you have a concussion, but better safe than prematurely drugged."

Daisy slowly pushed herself to her feet and sat down on the couch. "Can't we just go home? It's cold in here." Daisy looked around the room. "Where is Brian?"

"He was outside waiting for the ambulance and the rest of his team. He let me in." As if on cue they heard the door open again and two EMTs came into the room.

Daisy said, "I'm fine. You don't need to be here."

The taller of the two men said, "Probably not, but since I am here, why don't I just check a couple of things. It'll only take a minute. My name's Chad, by the way." Daisy sat still as Chad checked her pupils, took her blood pressure and pulse. "Do you know where you are?"

She snapped. "Of course, I do. I am in Holly Hill Mansion where someone bopped me on the head and stuffed me in the elevator. My name is Daisy Forrest and what I really need is a painkiller and a good night's sleep."

Chad smiled as he got to his feet. "You may have a mild concussion. I'd like to take you to the hospital where you can be observed."

"No way am I going to the hospital. I'm going home where Nurses Ratchet and Nightingale can observe me all they want."

Angela touched Chad's arm and said, "She'll be fine. I know what to look for and we will get her to the emergency room if we need to. She'll rest better at home. Don't you think?"

He shrugged his shoulders. "It's your call."

The paramedics were packing up when Daisy noticed Brian leaning against a sideboard watching. She said, "You shouldn't be touching the furniture. It's very old."

He stood up straight. "And you shouldn't have been here alone, much less snooping around murder scenes!"

"Excuse me?"

"Uh-oh. This is not good," said Rose.

But Brian continued, "Daisy, I asked you not to get involved. I told you to leave detecting to the professionals. You could have been killed. What were you thinking?"

She waited a moment before replying. She slowly got up and grabbed her purse, "I'm thinking that I don't like being talked to like I'm six. I am going home. If you want to pepper me with questions, you can just wait. I have a headache and my feet hurt. And right at this moment, I don't want to talk to you."

"You may not want to talk to me, but I need to know

what happened tonight."

"Just like I told my friend Chad. Someone hit me on the head. When I woke up I was lying on the floor of the elevator with my head on a pillow which is really pretty odd, if you think about it. I couldn't find my phone, so I blew my nose, ate a granola bar and waited to be yelled at by you. Altogether, it was not my idea of a great way to spend an evening."

Brian started to say something, but Angela stopped him. "Really Brian, maybe it's best to wait until everyone is a bit calmer. Daisy can go home and you can come by tomorrow and take her statement when she's feeling better."

He hesitated, but then said, "All right. I'll be over in the morning."

"Rose, could you drive my car home? My driving wouldn't be such a hot idea right now."

"Sorry," said Brian. "We need to check the car for fingerprints, but I'll get it back to you as soon as I can."

"My car! Why? It wasn't stuffed in the elevator."

"No, but whoever hit you, apparently drove it away and brought it back."

"Well, isn't that just marvy!"

Daisy, home at last, wrapped her flannel robe around her and snuggled in her chair. The Tylenol she had taken was beginning to do its job and she and Angela were sipping hot chocolate with marshmallows when Rose returned from seeing Peter out.

"Why didn't you just tell Brian what happened?" Rose asked.

"Hmm?" Daisy yawned. "I didn't like his tone. He sounded a lot like a policeman I know."

"Well, he is a policeman and he was upset. He was afraid you were dead."

"Tough walnuts. That's no excuse to be mean and

accuse me of things. I was not snooping and I wasn't alone. I'm not a total idiot. The caterers were still there cleaning up."

"I don't understand why someone would attack you." Angela said. "If he or she wanted to ransack the house, he or she could have waited until you left. You're sure you weren't doing a little investigative work? Peeking in closets or checking under rugs? You had quite a bump on the head. You may have forgotten."

Daisy shook her head. "I'm sure I wasn't nosing around. I was exhausted and all I wanted to do was lock up and get out of there."

"Well, what, exactly, were you doing when you were attacked?"

"I'd just finished shutting down the house and I went to the dining room to get my purse. I sat down for a moment to take my shoes off before heading home and..."

"And what?"

"Give me a minute. My headache's mostly gone, but everything is still a little fuzzy." She sat up straight in her chair and sipped her drink. "I got my purse from under the couch, I sat down - and then someone hit me on the head."

"That can't be right," Rose said. "You were hit on the back of your head. You must have had your back to the little piss-ant when he hit you or you'd have seen him. So you couldn't have been sitting down."

Daisy rubbed her temples and shook her head. "I don't know."

Angela rubbed Daisy's back. "Relax darling. Let it come back on its own."

The three of them sat in silence. Finally, Rose said, "Well, it's almost dawn. We should probably try to get some sleep."

She got up and stretched. Angela said, "You

dropped an earring, hon." Rose felt her ear, looked around on the floor, then stuck her hand into the crevice of the couch cushions and pulled it out.

Daisy shouted, "That's it!" as she jumped out her chair. Then she grabbed her head, sat back down, and put the ice pack back on again. "I shouldn't have done that."

"What are you talking about? What shouldn't you have done?" asked Rose.

"Jumped up like that. It hurts. But I just remembered what happened. Something was under the cushion. I stood up and pulled it out. I think it was an old diary. It had that spidery writing that comes from using a quill pen. I hadn't read much when someone felt it necessary to crack me on the head and everything went black. And then Sophia seemed to be telling me something about it."

"Was Sophia in the elevator?"

"No. She was in my dream." Daisy told them about the odd dream she had.

Angela agreed. "You're right. Sophia is clearly trying to tell you something. Now we just have to figure out what."

"I don't. Not right now, anyway," said Rose. "I need to get some sleep and so do both of you, especially Daisy. You should have been in bed hours ago."

Angela got up and took the mugs to the kitchen. "You're right. This will all keep 'til the morning."

Angela was up and out by eight o'clock. She left a note for the girls saying she needed to get back to Percy, and that she would call later, so they could figure out the dream and reschedule the tunnel investigation.

The phone started ringing at ten o'clock. A couple of reporters wanting statements. Adele Long checking to make sure Daisy was all right. Brian called to say he'd be there at noon. And Len Rutherford called to say he heard about the attack and wanted to come by later in the day.

At eleven there was knocking on the front door. Daisy said, "Brian's early." But Rose came back from answering it followed by a lovely young woman. "Daisy, this is Maisie Bailey from the Bulletin. She'd like a word." Dressed in a bright green wool suit and matching heals, Maisie Bailey looked more like a rising young lawyer, than a reporter.

Daisy smiled, "Well, you're definitely an improvement over the last reporter from the Bulletin. And I love your accent. Jamaica?"

Maisie laughed. "Indeed. I came over five years ago to attend the University of Maryland."

"And you stayed?"

"Yes. I may go back some day, but for now I am enjoying life here in the States."

Rose put a pot of tea and mugs on the table and a coffee cake. "Tea?"

"No, thank you." She turned to Daisy and said, "Do you mind talking to me about last night?"

Daisy sipped her tea thoughtfully. Finally, she said, "I'm not sure how much I should say. I don't want to scare people away from coming to Holly Hill."

"But you know someone is going to report on this. It isn't every day a murder takes place in a historic home and then the tour guide who found him gets attacked while on the job. It might as well be a friendly reporter," she smiled charmingly, "like me."

Daisy laughed. "There isn't really much to tell. The police can give you more information than I can."

"Whatever you can tell me would be wonderful."

Daisy gave a brief rundown of the night before. She didn't mention the diary or the tunnels. "I have no idea why someone wanted to put me in that elevator."

"Well, what about finding the dead man? Tell me about that."

"I'm sorry. The police have asked me not to talk about it."

Maisie said, "I've read about you and Rose. You seem to have a knack of solving crimes. Are you investigating this one?"

Daisy and Rose looked at each other. Daisy said, "I wouldn't go that far. We don't really investigate. Things just kind of land in our laps sometime. But leave your card. If we come up with anything good, I'll give you an exclusive."

An hour later, a clearly angry Brian Hathaway was sitting across from Daisy. "I don't understand why someone would attack you if you weren't doing anything."

Daisy rubbed her temples. "I told you. I sat on the sofa. I found what I think was an old diary. I got whacked on the head and shoved in the elevator. I've got the lump to prove it."

"Just where is this diary?"

"I hid it in the elevator while I was unconscious! How should I know? I presume the bad guy didn't want me to read it, so he took it."

"What I don't understand is why, knowing there's a killer on the loose, you were creeping around that mansion alone."

"I wasn't creeping around and I wasn't alone. The caterers were still outside." She put a hand to her head and said, "And, if you want to get technical, the head basher was hanging around, too."

"That's another thing. I want to know how is this guy getting in and out of the house without being seen? The caterers said no one came out after eleven. They checked the doors before they left at midnight and everything was locked. They assumed you'd already gone. So just how did your head basher get out?" He glared at her. "Daisy, there's something you're not telling me. What is it?"

She glared back. "Well, I had a dream while I was unconscious. Sophia was telling me something important and little clowns with shovels were going in and out of the mansion. And I think Sophia's daughter was there."

He said, "Daisy, when you're ready to get serious about this, let me know." Her eyes filled with tears and she said, "I'm tired and my head aches. I think you should go."

He got up and turned to leave, but then he turned back and kissed her on the top of her head. "I'm sorry, I shouldn't get mad at you, but you scared the hell out of me. You could have been killed."

"Well, I wasn't. And I do think Sophia is trying to tell me something."

"Look, I know you believe in that stuff, but I need concrete facts, not ghosts and dreams." He took her hand and smiled. "I think we should talk when you're feeling better. How about dinner Friday?"

She squeezed his hand and said, "I'd like that." She hesitated, then came to a decision. "You know, Brian, it's not only dreams..." She was just on the verge of telling him about the tunnels when Malcolm flew into the room and attached himself to Brian's leg. Brian laughed, unhitched the dog, and said, "I've got to get going. You get some rest and if you think of anything else about last night, even a message from the ghost, call me."

Chapter Eighteen

Daisy yawned. "Let's take a walk or something. I need some air."

"What you need is a long nap," said Rose. "Go lie down. I'll field calls for you." The phone had been ringing off the hook. The Old Towne grapevine had been hard at work and everyone and his mother wanted to get the inside story on the attempted murder of one of their own.

"I don't think I could sleep right now and I'd really like to get out of here for a while." She thought for a minute, then said, "I know. We don't have our pumpkins yet and Halloween is next weekend. I don't know what's wrong with me this year. I haven't even put the Indian corn on the door!"

Rose looked closely at her sister. "How's the headache?"

"Gone. I wouldn't want anyone patting me on the head just now and I still feel a little fuzzy, but I know some fresh air will help. You drive. I'll be fine."

"Okay. If you promise to take it easy."

"Oh, I will. We can get our gourds and then stop for an early dinner. I'll be tucked up in bed by nine like a good little patient."

They left Old Towne and headed out Central Avenue going east. Maryland on an October afternoon is hard to beat as the autumn sun shines through trees painted glorious shades of red, orange and yellow and the breeze holds just a hint of the winter to come.

Rose opened the sun roof and turned on the music. As they sang along with Whitney Houston Daisy felt truly relaxed for the first time since finding Wally's body.

They pulled into Queen Anne Farm and had to hunt for a parking place. Daisy said, "We should have come weeks ago. I'll bet there's nothing left."

But they were in luck. It had been a bumper year and the selection of bright orange jack-o-lantern pumpkins, beautiful heirloom gourds, and Indian corn was abundant. They spent a pleasant hour wandering the pumpkin patch. Daisy insisted that they take a hayride and walk through the corn maze. They fed goats and watched little kids have their faces painted.

Finally, the trunk and back seat were stuffed with enough pumpkins and gourds to decorate several houses, apples, apple cider and apple butter, six large chrysanthemums, and door decorations. Daisy wanted to get a bundles of corn stalks, but Rose pointed out that there was no more room. "We have to fit ourselves in there, too."

Rose put the last of the pumpkins in the trunk just as the sun was starting to set in the western sky casting a dazzling glare. She reached into her jacket pocket and pulled out her sunglasses and an orange handkerchief that was caught in the hinge.

Daisy said, "What's that?"

Rose tossed it on the seat and shrugged. "I don't know. It was in my pocket."

Daisy picked it up. "I'm sure I've seen this before. Where did you get it?"

She looked at it. "I have no idea. It's not mine."

Just then Daisy's cell rang. It was Len Rutherford saying he had stopped by the house and left something for her on the back porch. "It's a home remedy, good for what ails you. I feel like it's the least I can do. If I hadn't left early, you would never have been there by yourself."

"Len, it's not your fault. How are you feeling, anyway?"

"I'm okay. I must have eaten something that disagreed with me. Anyway, I'm glad you're feeling better. I'm calling an emergency board meeting for Tuesday evening to talk about how to handle this whole mess. We may need to close for a while. Do you think you'll be able to make it?"

"I'll be there. You could be right about closing, but I sure hope not."

They were home and settled in the living room watching an old Cary Grant movie by nine. At eleven Rose got up to let the dumb chums out for the night. She came back up the kitchen stairs carrying a small shopping bag.

Daisy asked, "What's that?"

Rose peeked in and pulled out a mason jar filled with some sort of liquid. "I think it must be the cure-all Len brought over. It was sitting on the porch near the door." She reached back into the bag and pulled out a piece of paper and read. "Yes. Len says this is his mother's recipe. Cures everything from the common cold to athlete's foot."

"I'm not sure what good it could do for a lump on the head. Anyway, I'm not drinking something that's been sitting outside all day." She looked at it. "Besides, it looks gross."

"It sure does." Rose stuck it the refrigerator. "Let's hit the sack. We both could use some sleep."

As they were closed Mondays, Rose spent the morning catching up on paperwork, paying bills, and dusting shelves.

Daisy spent it carving pumpkins and decorating. By

noon two jack-o'-lanterns - one scary face, one happy face - sat on either side of the shop door. Three stenciled pumpkins - a cute little dog in a top hat, another little dog in a wizard's hat, and a scary cat riding a broomstick - sat on their mantle. Indian corn was hanging on every door and huge golden chrysanthemums and heirloom gourds adorned the porch steps.

Angela and Percy came by after lunch to check on Daisy. "I love it! Malcolm, Percy and Roscoe right there on the mantle." She looked her daughter over and asked, "How do you really feel? You must be a bit better to have done all this work."

"Fine. The lump is still a little tender, but I managed to wash my hair today without screaming. Sit down. I just made a pot of tea and I have some good Irish cheddar to go with it. Have you decided on a costume for Saturday?"

"Yes, I have and it's a secret. Now, where is Rose? I want to go over our plan to search the tunnel."

Rose came up the kitchen staircase carrying Roscoe. She put the cat down gently and grabbed a mug. "We're not really going to do this tunnel thing, are we?"

Angela said, "I think we must, dear."

"What must we do?" Dickie Forrest burst into the kitchen.

Angela's hand jerked and she spilled her tea. "Dick Forrest! Have you ever heard of knocking? And why are you stalking me?"

"I am not stalking you. I heard all about Daisy's big adventure the other night and wanted to make sure she's all right. I am stunned that you didn't see fit to call me right away. I had to hear about it from Len. I felt like an idiot, being the last to know my own daughter was in dire peril."

"I was not in dire peril. I knew somebody would find me sooner or later. And I'm just fine now."

"So you say. You don't look so good to me."

"Gee, thanks. That certainly makes me feel better. I hope this will be a short visit. I need my rest."

"Daisy May, don't get on your high horse. I'm your father and I'm concerned about you. Someone hit you in the head with that thing and you could have been killed."

"What thing? How do you know what he hit me with, Dad?"

Dickie stammered. "I don't, but it had to be something. I do know that you're very lucky. If he had hit you any harder, you'd have been a goner."

"I'm well aware of that. Now why are you here?"

"We need answers. I was thinking that we never succeeded in getting in touch with the other side and your friendly ghost might know who is doing this and why, so…" He reached into his pocket and brought out a deck of cards. "I am going to deal the Tarot cards and read your fortune! How about that?"

The three women burst out laughing. Angela said, "What in the name of the King of Cups do you know about Tarot cards?"

"Plenty. The Ouija told me to try the Tarot. I may not know the ins and outs of what beats what, but I've got a good sense about the meanings of the cards. I'll set up right here." He swept the newspaper, a small pile of folded tea towels, and the cat off the dining room table with one arm. Then he opened the deck and started shuffling. Roscoe glared at him and actually sniffed, then stalked off to the kitchen.

"Rose June, Angie, Daisy May take your seats. Okay now, let me concentrate." He dealt each of them five cards. He turned his over. "Hey, look at that. I got a straight. That means I'm going to have an improvement in my love life. Angie, you turn yours."

Angela gave him a look. "I've never had a Tarot reading, but I'm just about positive this is not the way it's done."

Dickie said, "Well, it's the way I do it. Just turn them over."

"Anything to get you out of here." She turned her cards – the Lovers, Wheel of Fortune, Judgement, the King and Queen of Cups.

Dickie almost jumped out of his seat. "Angie, this means forgiveness and new beginnings. See, the Lovers and the King and Queen. I think it means you and me, back together again."

"Well, my dimpled dumpling, I think it means you're a few marbles short of a quarry. And don't call me Angie."

"Angela. You've become a very negative person. Did you know that? Very negative. Okay, Daisy. Turn your cards. Let's see if you can beat my straight."

As she turned her cards Daisy said, "Dad, you do realize this is not poker."

"Of course, it's not poker. It's an ancient form of truth telling. What have you got?" He studied her cards - Death, the Fool, the Hanged man, the Magician, and the Ace of Cups. "Well, this is clear as day. You're in for big changes and disaster, or maybe, new beginnings. I mean, that Hanged Man can't be good, can it? Or Death. I know the book said they just mean making changes in your life, but what if those changes are for the worse? Hmm."

Rose patted him on the head. "Dad, you have no idea at all what you're doing, do you?"

"Well, Ouija wasn't too specific about how this works. I think we'd do better just to get the board out again."

Angela gathered the cards and stuck them in his

pocket. Then she took him by the arm and said, "No Ouija today. The girls and I have better things to do. You know, Dickie, your half-witted idiot routine isn't particularly endearing. Time to go."

After Angela had seen Dickie drive off she came back up the stairs and said, "Now that he's gone, let's get down to business. When do you want to search the tunnel?"

Rose said, "Mother, I think this has gone far enough. We need to tell the police about the tunnel and let them handle it."

Angela looked at Daisy. "What do you think?"

"I intend to tell Brian everything Friday when we go out. I don't see why I shouldn't have all the facts to give him when I do."

"Absolutely right! Rose, if we can find the entrance in the mansion, then we save Brian a lot of work. So when do we do this?"

"Len has called an emergency staff meeting for tomorrow night," said Daisy. "You both come to the meeting and we'll go afterward."

Angela nodded. "Wonderful. That's settled."

Rose sighed loudly and said, "I can't believe we're going to do this. I need a drink. Maybe a little something would dull this very bad feeling I have about breaking into a haunted house to look for murderers. Anyone join me?"

"That sounds lovely," said Angela. "I don't know why you think this is a bad idea. We'll be together. What could possibly happen?"

"I can't imagine." Rose went into the kitchen and came back a few minutes later with three glasses filled with a fizzy pink mixture. "I call it the B&E. Cheers!"

Angela sipped. "Very nice. Now about this dream you had, Daisy. I'm not sure it was just a dream. I think Sophia was trying to tell you something. Tell us again what you saw."

"I was reading a book with spidery writing and a map. There were clowns with shovels. And Sophia and another woman were standing in the woods. I'm sure it was her daughter, Amelia."

"Could the diary have been Sophia's? I think it's clear that the clowns were digging the tunnel. But I don't know why Amelia was asking her mother if she could come home."

"I don't think she was," said Rose. "There was another daughter, remember. Matilda. I've been trying to do a little research into the Longs on-line. The family in the U.S. is pretty straight forward. And I've just gotten as far as Matilda leaving for England, but I ran into a dead end there. I might run over to Sally's this week if she has time. She's better at all this ancestry stuff than I am."

"Good idea. Mother, do you think Adele knows anything about this?"

"I've asked her about the family and she was told that Matilda died not long after she got to England. That's all she would say. She didn't want to discuss it. I think she feels guilty about the way Matilda was treated."

"Well, that's silly," said Daisy. "She had nothing to do with that. Anyway, I wonder if that was Matilda in the dream asking to come home."

Rose shrugged. "As sad as that sounds, what does that have to do with us?"

"I don't know. Maybe nothing. Maybe it was just a weird dream. The result of being conked on the head. Speaking of which, Mother, you don't think Dad would do that, do you?"

"Daisy! Of course not. Why would you ask that?"

"Because he sounded like he knew something about it. And he's been acting so odd since he got here and we know he's up to something."

"Well, he's not up to hurting his girls. He may be a lot of things, but he has never been violent and he does love you in his own strange way." She stood up and took the cups to the sink. "Next up, are you ready for this party you're having on Saturday? Who's coming?"

Daisy said, "The usual suspects – Peter, Marc, Sally, Tonya and Tom, and Brian, I hope."

"What can I do?"

Rose said, "Just enjoy yourself. We've got it all under control. Daisy's decorated. We're having it catered this year and we've ordered enough food to sink a ship. And I've created a signature cocktail. It should be fun."

"Did you invite your father?"

"No. He invited himself. He told me he's coming as the Mad Hatter."

"Well, I am certainly not coming as Alice!"

Chapter Nineteen

"Mother, this looks ridiculous. I really don't see why we all had to wear black." Rose parked the car in the Visitor Center lot and got out. "We look a bit suspicious, don't you think?"

"Not at all. Everyone looks good in black."

Daisy laughed and said, "I have to agree with Rose on this one. Not that I care, but someone might think we're some sort of cat burglars."

Angela said, "At least we're well dressed cat burglars, though I think second-story women sounds more romantic."

They got to the Carriage House just as Len Rutherford was saying, "Would everyone please sit down so we can get started?" He stood at the head of the table and surveyed the audience. In addition to the Board and most of the docents there were a few others present. Rose and Angela, Adele and Leo, and a number of people from the neighborhood.

"This meeting was only meant for the staff, but I see that we have quite a few guests this evening. I suppose with all that's been going on that's to be expected. Karen, will you take the attendance and minutes?"

Karen Casey stood and waved her clipboard in the air. "Of course. I'm passing the sign-in sheet around. Please make sure to, you know, sign-in before you leave."

Len continued, "First, the good news. Our Gothic Evening was a huge success. I think Wally would have been pleased. Over two hundred tickets were sold and I've gotten a lot of very positive feedback. I understand the catering was quite an improvement over last year and Mr. Poe was especially well-liked. He has already promised to play the part again next year.

"However, as most of you know we had a near tragedy that same evening. For anyone who hasn't heard yet, one of our docents, Daisy Forrest, was attacked Saturday night after everyone had left. Luckily, she wasn't badly hurt, but it could have been much worse."

All eyes turned to Daisy who blushed, then said, "No need to worry about me. I'm fine. It was just a bit scary."

Leo Walters asked, "Daisy, do you remember any of it? Did you see who attacked you? You could still be in danger."

"No. Well, yes, I think I remember most of it, but I never saw anyone. The snake snuck up behind me. When I came to I was alone in the elevator."

"You're certain you don't remember anything about this guy? You didn't hear footsteps or smell aftershave or cigar smoke? Nothing you could recognize?"

Daisy looked at him oddly. "No. I didn't see, hear, or smell him. Anyway, I would have told the police right away. And I know we keep saying him, but it could have been a woman."

Leo took his glasses off, pulled a red cloth from his pocket and wiped them. "That's unfortunate. Exactly what are the police doing? I find this is totally unacceptable. My aunt is alone here. Anything could happen to her."

Adele patted his hand. "Leo is being overprotective. I'm fine and not at all afraid."

"I can't help but worry about you, Aunt Adele. We don't know what this guy," he looked pointedly at Daisy, "- or woman – is after, do we? Len, what do the police

166

say?"

"They think the same person who killed Wally Stone was responsible for attacking Daisy. Of course, I'm not privy to the investigation, but I got the distinct feeling that they have no idea who this person is. The question for us here tonight is how do we handle this situation?"

Joy Phillips, Holly Hill's oldest docent, clocking in at seventy-two with twenty years on the job, said, "I think we should close until they catch him. I know I can't be the only one who doesn't feel safe here anymore."

Alice Joseph nodded. "I tend to agree with you."

"Len, I think that's kind of drastic," said Daisy. "Couldn't we just make sure that at least two docents are always together? Maybe we could install cameras in the house."

"I'm working with Park and Planning to find the funds for upgrades in security, but it will take a while. And we can't take the chance of another attack."

After a half hour of discussion Len said, "I've made my decision. We will close this weekend, then meet again in a week. Maybe by then, the villain will have been found."

Daisy, Rose and Angela left with the others. They got into Rose's car and were pulling out of the lot when Angela said, "Isn't that your father's car?"

A red Mustang sat in the far corner of the lot. Daisy said, "It could be."

"He's trailing me. I know it. Do you think he overheard us plan this mission?"

Rose looked at the car. "I can't think why he'd care. Anyway, he's not in the car and he wasn't at the meeting. It probably belongs to someone else."

Angela said, "It better had. If I find out that he's been lurking, he going to wish he hadn't."

They drove around the corner into the neighborhood

behind the mansion to wait until everything was shut down for the night.

Angela reached into the back seat and opened a picnic basket. She pulled out sandwiches, a thermos of tea, and paper cups. "I thought we'd need a little sustenance for our adventure."

"Did Brian say when you'll get your car back?" Rose asked.

"I think tomorrow. We haven't really had time to chat. I can't figure out why this guy took my car and then brought it back. Why not dump it somewhere else?"

"I've been thinking about that. I believe he wanted to make sure you were found. And that makes me wonder if whoever is doing this really meant to kill Wally." Rose took a sip of tea and coughed. "Mother, what's in this?"

"Just a hint of cognac. It's a chilly evening."

"Good thinking, Mom." Daisy drank her tea and thought. "Rose, you could be right. He could have killed me, but he didn't. And he put that pillow under my head, which was weird if he wanted me dead. Maybe poor old Wally was just unlucky and had a softer head than I do."

"Or maybe I'm wrong. Maybe Wally saw this guy or figured out who it was and had to be killed."

"That could be it. I'm glad I didn't see anyone. Hey, did either of you think Leo was a little too interested in whether I saw anything and what I remembered?"

Angela thought a moment. "Not really. I think it's natural. He's clearly worried about Adele and wants answers."

"It seemed like more than that to me. He was doing something this evening. I can't put my finger on it. Oh, well," she looked at her watch. "Time to go."

Armed with brand new Maglite ML300Ls each in an attractive royal blue Daisy had ordered for the occasion, they left the car where it was and walked back to the mansion. The Mustang was gone from the parking lot. As they skirted the trees along the drive they glanced across the lawn at Adele's darkened cottage, then crept to the east wing door.

Daisy unlocked it and the three women slipped in. After disarming the alarm, she relocked the door and reset the alarm. "No one will ever know we've been here."

Rose asked, "Why do you still have the key?"

"I don't."

"What? Sophia just unlocked the door for us?"

"Of course not. This is not an official key. I had one made. Just in case."

"Just in case, my asp! You had this planned weeks ago."

They were walking slowly down the dark, silent hall toward the basement staircase. As they passed the dining room the mantel clock chimed loudly causing Rose to jump and knock into a large urn that sat on a pedestal at the door to the salon. She managed to catch it just before it fell.

Daisy whispered, "Would you relax? And watch where you're going. You could have broken my foot with that thing."

"I just hope we don't all get something broken. You know, this is not the brightest idea we've had. There's still a murderer on the loose who likes to haunt this place, remember. So, in case we're killed, I'd just like it on the record that I think we should have let Brian and the police handle it."

Daisy smiled sweetly and said, "You can go back to the car if you want. Mother and I will be fine."

"I'm not leaving you alone. You need someone with more than half a brain. No offense, Mother. Okay, if we're doing this, let's get it over with."

They got to the basement door and used their

flashlights to guide them down the narrow staircase. Daisy led the way to the doors of the storage area. "Be careful. The floor's uneven and the ceiling's low in places."

Rose ducked just in time to miss hitting her head on an overhead beam and muttered, "Why am I here?"

The storage room was large, about twenty feet square, filled with moldy furniture, folding tables and chairs, a small refrigerator, shelves lined with boxes of Christmas decorations and Civil War reenactment paraphernalia.

They moved slowly shining their lights around the room. Suddenly Rose let out a scream and pulled Daisy and Angela down behind a box of old brochures. She whispered frantically, "There's someone in here!"

Angela flashed her beam into the corner and said, "Sweetheart, I believe that's a mannequin dressed as Father Christmas."

"Rose, get a grip. And keep it down. You'll wake the dead," said Daisy.

"That would be wonderful, sweetheart. Sophia can probably tell us right where to look."

They were standing at the back of the room staring at the wall. It was lined with shelves except for one spot that had just a few boxes piled up.

Daisy said, "I'm sure this is where the paint smear was." They moved the boxes, but there was no sign of a door or loose bricks.

Rose looked around. "You only saw it for a moment. Maybe it's behind one of the shelves." As Rose shone her light over the closest shelf, it started flickering. She said, "What's wrong with this thing. You did put new batteries in, didn't you?"

"Of course. These are brand new Maglites."

Rose turned hers off, then back on. The beam held steady when she pointed it to the spot where Daisy thought she saw the paint, but flickered again when she pointed it toward the shelf. Daisy and Angela did the same. The lights held steady at the same point along the wall.

Rose murmured, "This is eerie."

"I think you did wake the dead and this is Sophia directing us," said Daisy. "Adele told us she loves lights and things."

Angela moved closer to the wall and ran her hands over it. As she did the brick floor creaked. "That's odd." She crouched down and shone her flashlight on the ground. The beam became a hot pink.

Rose whispered, "Holy halogen light bulbs!"

Daisy whispered back, "LED actually, but spooky none the less."

Angela pointed. "Look at this. I think these bricks are loose." She tried to pry one up, but it was didn't budge. "We need a crowbar or something."

Daisy hunted around the room and came up with a small hammer. "See if this will work."

Angela studied the surface and found a spot where the mortar seemed to have had chipped away. She wedged the claw into the slot and pulled. Nothing happened. Daisy leaned against the wall just as Angela tried again. Suddenly a whole portion of the floor popped up as a piece and slid away from her, depositing Angela abruptly on her rear end.

"Mother are you all right?" Angela sprang to her feet, dusted herself off and said, "Fine. What did we find?"

Daisy backed up and fingered a small brick that was now indented about a half inch into the wall. "I believe we found the mechanism that opens this hidden door." Angela rubbed her bottom and said, "I wish we had found it a bit earlier."

Daisy squatted on the floor and examined the lid. "This is really ingenious. These bricks have been mounted on a piece of wood that fits into the floor like a large tile. See, it's hinged like a hatch on a boat with a handle on the underside so we can slide it back in place when we go down."

Rose said, "When we go down where exactly?"

"Down there." The three of them shone their flashlights into the hole they had just uncovered. A short ladder was propped against the wall. "This must be the way our little pit viper is getting in and out of the mansion. So, what do you think? Shall we?"

Rose sighed loudly, but followed her mother as she climbed down the ladder. Daisy was last. "I'm closing this baby up. Flashlights on?" She pulled the covering over the hole. It settled into place with a loud thud.

They found themselves standing in a passage almost six feet high and about three feet across. It was cold, dark, and claustrophobic. Rose shivered and said, "I don't think you should have closed the door. Can we get it open again?"

"Sure we can. You worry too much." Daisy shone her light at the ceiling and the walls. "No cobwebs and the hinges were well oiled. This has definitely been used recently."

They moved slowly as they were not able to see more than a few feet in front of them. Angela said, "Keep your eyes sharp. Maybe we'll find a clue."

Rose shone her light behind her. "Well, there aren't any footprints. The dirt's packed too hard to leave an impression. Where do you think this leads?"

Angela pulled a compass out of her pocket. "We're heading south. The kitchen is toward the east, isn't it?"

"It is," said Daisy. "This must be a different tunnel. Maybe they connect somewhere, but Rose and I didn't find any opening the other day."

They moved slowly along the tunnel. The floor was uneven, as was the ceiling. At one point, Rose bumped her head and stumbled forward. "Ouch!" As she pushed herself up she had a deja-vu moment. "Daisy, hold it a minute."

"Are you hurt?"

"No, I'm all right, but I just remembered something. Do you recall that little piece of orange cloth?"

"What cloth?"

"You know, that handkerchief thing. It was bright orange. I found in my pocket when we were at the pumpkin patch."

Daisy thought a minute. "Yeah. What about it?"

"Well, when we were in the kitchen tunnel, I tripped because you forgot new batteries and the flashlight died and I couldn't see anything…"

"You have to let these things go, Rose."

"I was just saying. Anyway, I've remembered how it got in my jacket. It was on the ground and I picked it up and stuck it in my pocket."

Daisy pictured sitting in the car fingering the silky fabric. "Wow. That's weird. You know, I had the feeling that I've seen it before." She closed her eyes. "Shoot. It's right there, but I can't grab it. And I think it might be important. That piece of cloth probably belongs to the killer."

"We don't know that. I could have been anyone's."

"Exactly how many people do you think are roaming these tunnels?"

Rose looked around and shuddered. "Come on, let's see where this ends and get out of here."

They came to a wall, finally, with another ladder propped against it. Daisy climbed up. "It's another trap door, but I don't see any hinges here. If I can just push up with these handles." The door didn't budge. "I can't do it. Rose, you try."

Rose pushed a few times, then tried a different angle. Nothing moved.

Daisy said, "Try kicking it."

"What?"

"Wedge your feet against it."

"No way in hell. You wedge your feet against it!" She pounded on the panel. "I'll bet it's locked. Well, I certainly hope we can get out the other end or we could be in real trouble. I knew this was a bad idea."

"Oh, for heaven sakes. Get down from there." Angela climbed the ladder and gripped the handles. Then she took a deep breath and - whoosh - the door popped open and they felt the night breeze on their faces. She grabbed the edge of the hole, kicked the ladder away and pulled herself out. She stood and watched as Daisy and Rose righted the ladder and climbed out a bit less gracefully.

"Mother, how did you do that?"

"I do ten burpees every day to keep me strong. It's the complete body work-out."

They found themselves in the middle of what might have been the remains of a shallow well or some sort of igloo. A crumbling brick wall about five feet high, two feet of it above ground, tapered away at the north side to ground level. Rose said, "What is this place?"

"It's the ruins of an old ice house. Well, now we know how our mystery man, who may or may not be the owner of a bright orange handkerchief, is getting in and out."

Rose looked at her sister. "Daisy, you need to tell Brian about this."

"I know I do. I'll call him in the morning and confess everything. Well, maybe not everything. We'd better cover this up again." She and Rose picked up the lid, a piece of wood coated with gravel and dirt, and fixed it over the entrance.

While Daisy and Rose were fitting the cover back in place, Angela looked around the ruins. "It must have been romantic having a tunnel to an ice house. This could have been a place for lovers' trysts. Sneaking out of the house to meet your beloved."

"More likely a way for old Josiah to get away from creditors or someone he stiffed at poker. And I wonder how well it worked when it was filled with ice," said Rose.

Angela thought a minute. "I'll bet that's why there are two tunnels. One for winter and one for summer."

They hopped out of the ice house. Daisy brushed her hands and looked down into the well. "You'd never know it was there, would you?"

Angela heard scuffling and pointed her flashlight at an old tree stump. A small creature scurried out from a crack, disturbing a pile of dead leaves, and ran into the darkness. Something glinted in the moonlight. "What's that?" Angela brushed the leaves away with her foot, took the scarf from around her neck and picked an old iron off the ground.

Daisy looked at it. "I think that's one of ours. It belongs in the servants' hall display. What's it doing out here?"

"I think this might be what killed Wally." Rose pointed to a dark smudge on its side. "I'll bet that's blood. You wanted a clue, Mother. I think we have one. Do we leave it in place or take it with us?"

Angela wrapped it carefully in her scarf. "I think we have to take it with us. I'm afraid it might be gone by the time the police get here."

As they were walking through the woods Daisy stopped suddenly and whispered, "Listen."

"What are we listening for?"

"I heard something moving behind us."

Angela shone her flashlight into the trees. "I don't see anything. It was probably a little fox or, maybe, a deer. Let's keep going. It's getting chilly."

Daisy stared into the darkness, then turned and practically ran to the car.

Chapter Twenty

Daisy, Rose, and Angela sat silently sipping cocoa staring at the iron they had found propped in the middle of the kitchen table. It was almost midnight.

Daisy said, "I think we were being watched. And I know you're strong Mother, but Rose and I aren't exactly weaklings. We should have been able to push that trapdoor open. I think someone was standing on it and then hid in the woods."

Angela dunked biscotti into her cocoa. "Daisy, I think you're being a little melodramatic. How would this someone know we were in there and why would he let us out?"

"What if he didn't? Maybe it was a coincidence and the burglar just happened to be getting ready to go into the mansion again right as we were coming out."

"Ooh, that's creepy. I'd prefer to think it was Dad stalking Mother," said Rose.

"Me, too, and I guess it could have been, but I don't think it was. Damn! We should've gone back and blocked the entrance!"

Angela got up and said, "Well, we didn't and whoever it was, if it was anyone, he or she knows we found the way in. Maybe we scared him off. At any rate, it's time for bed. Dot and I have a costume fitting early in the morning. I don't want to be late."

At eight Wednesday morning, Daisy and Malcolm stared out the kitchen window watching a cold rain drench his play yard. "Looks like an indoor day for you, little guy."

Malcolm barked once, then moseyed over to his cozy little bed in the corner, circled five times and snuggled into it. Roscoe wandered in from the living room, lapped water from his bowl and joined Malcolm. Within seconds they were both snoring gently. Daisy looked at them wistfully. "I wish I could go back to bed, too. I think I'd rather sleep all day than make this call to Brian. Something tells me that he's not going to be particularly happy with what I have to tell him."

Rose came into the kitchen. "Talking to yourself again?"

"I was talking to Malcolm."

Rose looked at the sleeping dog. "I don't think he's interested. At any rate, I just watched the news and I think you're probably off the hook for this morning, at least. It looks like the world is going to hell in a hand basket and it's all hands on deck."

Daisy turned on the little kitchen television. Breaking news was on every channel. "Well, that's a first. This is actually breaking news." Two gunmen were holding the employees of a Hyattsville bank hostage. A twelve-car pile-up at rush hour on the John Hansen Highway at the Beltway had caused a massive traffic jam. Bomb threats had been called in to four local high schools. And to top it off there was a fire on Metro's Blue line.

"We live in a wonderful world, don't we? I'm glad we don't have to commute to work. I think I'll give Brian a try anyway." Daisy dialed Brian's number which went directly to voice mail. She left a short message and hung up. "Well, that's done."

"You didn't do anything!"

"I called. I can't help it if he didn't answer. I could hardly explain everything in a voice mail message."

"Have you decided what you're going to tell him?"

"Sort of. I'm hoping he won't be too mad. With all this going on today, maybe I should just wait until we go out Friday. I mean, what difference will one more day make? In person I can be much more charming than over the phone. And when you think about it, he had all the same clues that we had. He could have found the tunnel himself. He really should thank me."

"You keep telling yourself that."

They opened the shop at nine. The morning dragged on. By noon, the only person to have come in the door was the mailman. Daisy said, "Rose, we don't both need to be here. Why don't you take the afternoon off?"

"Are you sure? Tonya's not coming in today. Midterms this week. You'll be alone."

"If by some miracle we get busy, I'll call you."

"Okay then, I think I will. I've got to call the caterer and make sure everything is on track for Saturday. And I've got a couple of things I want to check on the computer. A nice rainy day is perfect for research."

"You have fun. I'm going to rearrange things in here to make room for that shipment of Christmas china we have coming next week."

By evening only one customer had come in to buy some hand-crafted soaps and bath oil. Daisy had rearranged and re-rearranged several displays and dusted every surface in the shop until the knot on her head was beginning to ache. At six she locked the door, turned the sign to closed, and trudged up the stairs.

Rose was still at the computer. "You look worn out. You should have called me."

"I'm fine. We only had one customer. My head's aching a bit, but mostly I'm bored." She got a glass of water and took two aspirin. She glanced over Rose's shoulder at the computer screen. "Find anything interesting?"

Rose grinned broadly. "I did. I think we might be related to Betsy Ross! How about that?"

"*The* Betsy Ross?"

"Well, *a* Betsy Ross. Could be the same one."

"I thought you were looking up the Long family."

"I was, but got side-tracked. This ancestry stuff is amazing. Sally and I are getting together tomorrow night so she can show me how to search further back. She has access to records in England."

"Do you know what you're looking for?"

"Kind of. I'm curious about Matilda. It was such a sad story how her family disowned her. I'd like to know if she had a happy life."

"Didn't Adele say she died shortly after moving to England?"

"I know. But maybe she didn't. That's just what her family thought. I want to find out just what happened to her. Did you hear from Brian?"

"He called to say he couldn't talk and he'd see me Friday. The mansion's closed. Nobody's in danger. So I think I'll just wait to tell him about the tunnel until then."

"Fraidy-cat."

"I prefer to consider myself judiciously self-protective."

Daisy had just finished a marinade and was taking chicken for dinner out of the refrigerator when Malcolm ran through the kitchen dragging something in his mouth with Roscoe close behind. "Where do you think you're going? No running in the house. Remember?" She scooped up Malcolm and took a bright orange handkerchief from him. "Where did you get this?"

She held the cloth in her hands and stared at it. "Boy, I know I've seen this before." And then it came to her. "Rose, get in here."

"What?" She saw what Daisy was holding and said,

"I thought I threw that away."

"Malcolm and Roscoe were playing with it. But, get this, I just remembered where I've seen it. Leo Walters uses these to clean his glasses. He had a red one at the meeting the other night. And I saw him use this one when he came here to dinner."

"Are you sure?"

"Positive. Leo must have been in the kitchen tunnel. I'll bet that door we came to leads to Adele's house."

"That would make sense. She and Leo must know about the tunnels. But why would he be using them? I can see him playing in them when he was a kid, maybe, but he's not ten anymore."

Daisy shook her head. "I don't know. Maybe he was searching for the silver or keeping watch over the mansion. Maybe he just a really weird guy who likes to play hide and seek."

"Or maybe he's the one who attacked you and killed Wally. You know, we just assume that the murder had to have something to do with someone looking for the silver. What if Leo had some grudge against Wally? He could have felt like he was cheated out of his estate when Adele sold it." Rose sighed. "Or maybe he's just a crazy nut person who got a taste for whacking people on the head."

"He was asking a lot of questions about whether I saw who hit me." Daisy slipped a chicken breast into a plastic bag and started pounding it with a wooden mallet. "Could you clean those potatoes? I thought I'd bake them while the chicken marinates."

"Sure." She got out the vegetable brush and scrubbed two good sized russets. As she pierced each one with the tip of a knife she said, "But I don't see Leo as a killer."

"Well, who did you see as a killer? Dad? I mean killers don't wear scarlet Ks embroidered on their shirts. I'm not sure what to think about Leo, but I'm not sure I trust him."

Chapter Twenty-One

Thursday the rain stopped and the sun came out. A steady flow of customers kept the sisters and Tonya busy all day. Finally, at five o'clock Rose locked the door and said, "Whew! That was crazy."

"Crazy good. I think this was our best day ever."

Tonya said, "If you don't mind, I've got a class at seven and I really need to scoot. And remember I'm off tomorrow."

Tonya was heading out when Rose asked, "Have you and Tom picked out your costumes for the party?"

"Yes. Not too original. We're coming as Raggedy Ann and Andy. You're sure it's all right if I'm off tomorrow?"

"Absolutely. We'll see you Saturday night."

Rose was setting the table and Daisy was making salad to go with the lasagna that was baking in the oven when Angela came by. She handed Rose a pumpkin filled with a beautiful arrangement of dried flowers. "For the party. You wouldn't let me cook, so I put this together."

"They're gorgeous. Absolutely perfect. Thank you, but you didn't need to bring them over tonight."

"I'm on my way to Adele's. She called and asked if I'd come over. She sounded a little upset."

"I wonder if it's got anything to do with Leo." Daisy told her mother about Leo and the orange cloth.

"I don't for one minute believe Leo would hurt

anyone. He's just not type."

"Sophia did tell us to beware of the lion and Leo means lion."

"I don't think that's what she meant at all. Rose probably got the message garbled."

Rose threw her hands up. "Don't bring me into this. I wasn't even aware I was saying it."

Angela said, "I know dear. It's just that sometimes the spirits get their wires crossed when speaking to non-dead people."

Daisy took the lasagna out of the oven. "That's true."

"Since when are the two of you experts on how spirits operate? Should I set a place for you, Mother?" asked Rose.

"No. Thank you darling, but I've already eaten and I left Percy in the car. Well, I'll just have to find a way to ask Adele why Leo might be roaming around those tunnels. Enjoy your dinner. It smells delicious. Call me if you need me."

After dinner Rose said she was going to Sally's to explore some more family ties. "I should be home by eleven or so."

"That's fine. Happy hunting."

By nine o'clock the warm autumn day had turned into a raw October night. The wind started gusting, rattling the windows of the old house, and the lights began to flicker. Thunder rumbled in the distance. Daisy felt uneasy and very alone. She checked the locks, locked the doggie door, and turned on the alarm. Malcolm and Roscoe seemed on edge, too. They couldn't settle down. Malcolm kept asking to go out, only to come right back in.

She had tried to get hold of Brian again, but he only had time for a quick hello. Marc called to say he was bringing a date to the party and ask if they needed him to do anything for Saturday night. They ended up chit-chatting for almost thirty minutes until her cell battery ran out.

Daisy turned on the TV, but nothing caught her attention. She combed the cat, put in a load of laundry, and pretended to work out with her dumb bells for a while. Finally, she decided a little baking would calm her down. She got out the milk, eggs, flour and sugar. "What do you think, guys, scones or muffins?" Roscoe twitched his tail and Malcolm gave a little bark. "Blueberry? Okay, blueberry muffins it is." She had just finished mixing when the land line rang. She looked at the clock. "Well, who could that be?" She grabbed the phone with her free hand.

"Daisy, it's Len Rutherford. Sorry to call so late, but we seem to have a problem up here at the mansion."

Daisy put down the spatula, wiped her hands, and said, "What's going on? Is Adele all right?"

"Oh, sorry, I didn't mean to scare you. She's fine. It's just that I was up here checking on things and someone has gotten in here again."

"You were checking on things at this time of night?"

"I figure that's when someone would be breaking in."

Daisy thought back to the night before and breathed a mental sigh of relief that he hadn't caught them exploring, thinking that it would be a bit difficult to explain. "Oh, I guess that does make sense."

"Well, some lights were on that shouldn't have been and when I tried the door, it was unlocked. I thought I saw Ms. Long's nephew walking into the woods and wondered if he had been inside. I think he's kind of an odd duck, so I checked the Dower house to make sure everything was all right. Ms. Long and your mother were having tea. They said they haven't seen anyone and that Leo doesn't have a key to the mansion."

"Did you call the police?"

"Yes. They're going to try to get someone out, but with this storm I don't know when they'll get here. Anyway, I was wondering if you could come up and help me figure out if anything is missing. You know the Holly Hill so much better than I do."

A crack of thunder suddenly shook the house and Daisy almost dropped the phone. "Can't it wait till tomorrow?"

"It could, but your mother is insisting on doing it herself now. And I can't stop her."

She had a vision of Leo hiding in the tunnel and Angela going to search for him. "All right. Give me half an hour. And tell my lunatic mother to wait till I get there."

She put the phone down just as another clap of thunder burst overhead and the lights went out. They came back on a second later, but when she tried to call Rose she found that the phone line was out.

"Okay guys. Roscoe, you stay here and hold down the fort. Malcolm, you're coming with me."

She quickly picked up the bowl of batter and shoved it into the refrigerator. As she did a mason jar filled with some dark, gooey liquid fell and broke when it hit the floor. "Dammit!"

Daisy side-stepped the mess that was slowly spreading on the tile, but Malcolm managed to walk right through it. He backed away leaving sticky paw prints on the floor. Daisy grabbed a damp paper towel and wiped his feet, then looked at the floor and sighed. "It'll just have to wait until I get home."

She snatched her cell from the charger and sent a quick text to Rose. "Urgent. Meet me at Adele's right away. I think Leo's the lion!!!"

Roscoe rubbed her leg and yipped. She checked the cell battery which was barely registering. "You know what? You're right. I'm leaving her a note, too, just in case the text didn't go through." She jotted a short message and put it on the mantel. She stroked the little cat's ears and said, "Roscoe, make sure Rose gets this."

Then she grabbed her anorak and Malcolm's rain coat and leash from the closet and the two of them headed into the storm.

Rose and Sally were sipping wine as thunder rumbled overhead. Sally had taken a tour of Ireland a while ago and had some fabulous pictures and some very funny stories about the trip. "Well, it was windy that afternoon. I now know what an Irish piper wears under his kilt and it isn't much!" They both laughed.

"I wonder if my father ever wears a kilt? That would be right up his alley." Rose told her about Dickie showing up out of the blue. "We still haven't figured out what he wants except that he insists on getting in touch with dead relatives. I know he's got some ulterior motive, but that got me thinking about all of our ancestors, so I've been trying to trace our family roots. I think we're related to Betsy Ross."

"That's pretty impressive."

"Not really. As far as I could tell John Claypoole, Betsy's third husband, had a sister who was married to some second cousin of mine who's about thirty times removed, if I've got this whole removed thing right. So, we actually aren't all that close. We don't even exchange Christmas cards."

Sally smiled, but then got serious and said, "Any more word on the murder? I missed the emergency meeting and haven't seen Daisy since she was attacked. I still can't believe she was the one who found Wally. You and she seem to attract dead bodies."

"Not our fault. We certainly don't look for them. At any rate, I don't think the police have gotten anywhere really. It's pretty scary having some lunatic running around."

"It sure is. If they don't catch him soon, I think a few of the docents will quit." Sally got up and handed Rose a folder. "Now take a look at this. When you told me you were looking into the Long family, I went ahead and did a little research on my own that I think you'll find interesting. I printed it out for you."

Rose looked over the pages briefly, then took her time and read them through. "So, Matilda didn't die shortly after she got to England. According to Adele, the family thought she had."

"Not only did she not die, she had two children and lived into her seventies."

"I see that. How did you find this out so easily? Didn't you have to ask for stuff from England?"

"Someone else had already done that."

"Can you tell who?"

"Yes. Keep reading."

Rose read out loud to herself. "Matilda married Louis Sutter. Their kids were Samuel and George. George married, okay, one son, no-not the son, his daughter. George's daughter, Mary, marries..." She stood up so quickly she spilled her wine. "Holy ancient ancestors! I've got to tell Daisy. I didn't see this coming."

She pulled out her phone and dialed Daisy's cell, but it went to voicemail. She tried the land line and got a busy signal.

"I'd better get home. This storm is just getting worse and I can't get Daisy on her cell. Sorry about the wine."

"Not a problem. Be careful, would you?"

"Always." She held up the folder. "Thanks for this." She ran to her car and got back to The Elms two minutes later. All the lights were on, but the place was empty. She saw the mess on the kitchen floor and got a sinking feeling in her stomach. She checked the bedrooms and the shop. She even ran down to the laundry room in the basement. She was standing in the living room in a near panic when Roscoe rubbed against her legs and meowed loudly. "I don't speak cat too well. Could you be a little more specific?" The cat jumped onto the mantel and knocked the note onto the floor. Rose looked at him in admiration. "I guess you can."

She read the note and swore under her breath. "She's got the wrong lion," and dashed back into the storm.

The rain was pouring down and Daisy could barely see the turn off for Holly Hill. She slowed to a crawl and braked in front of Adele's. The lights were on and the front door was open. She grabbed her Maglite and ran up to the porch and called out. No one answered. She stepped into the living room. "Adele? It's Daisy. Adele, is everything okay?" The only sound she heard was the ticking of the long clock.

She held her flashlight over her head like a club and quickly checked the rest of the rooms. A chair in the dining room was on its side and a vase was in pieces on the floor. Daisy turned to leave when she heard a soft mewing. She found Adele's cat, Amelia, cowering under the table. "What happened? Are you hurt?" The cat's frightened eyes looked up at Daisy and she ran from the room and dove under the sofa. Daisy said, "It'll be all right. You stay there. I'll find your friend."

She drove up to the mansion and saw that, here too, all the lights were on. As she pulled to a stop the downpour suddenly ended, but it wasn't particularly comforting. The heavy air felt electric and menacing. She put the leash on Malcolm and said, "Come on, big guy, we might have to save Mother."

Malcolm paused and let out a howl. Then he broke

free and ran into the hedge lining the driveway. "Malcolm, come back here. What do you think you're doing?"

He did come back, followed by a soaking wet Percy. He was limping and Daisy could see a trickle of blood on his white fur. "Percy!" She picked him up and checked him all over. A small lump was forming on his little head. "Oh my poor baby. Looks like Leo got you too." Percy gave two short yips. "I know sweetheart, but it's not too bad. We'll find Mother and then I'll fix you up. Come on, buddy, stick with us and you'll be fine."

They went to the east door which swung open when Daisy pushed on it. She walked in and stood in the hallway. Nobody was waiting for them. "Len said he couldn't stop Mother. Let's hope she hasn't gone into that tunnel alone or something stupid like that." Daisy called out, "Mother, Len, Adele, anyone? Where are you?"

There was no answer. She looked at Malcolm and Percy who were sitting on the stoop and said, "I want you two to wait in the butler's pantry. No sense all of us getting killed." They trotted in and followed her to the small room adjacent to the kitchen that was filled with Long family china. She opened the door and said, "In you go."

Malcolm looked at her and sniffed. Then he turned and started off down the hall. She whispered urgently, "Come on, Malcolm. This is no time to be difficult. Stay with Percy."

He came back and stared up at her as if to say, "I think you're crazy to go in there alone."

"I'll be fine." He didn't blink. "How's this? I'll holler if I'm in trouble." The little dog blinked, then shook himself and sat down next to Percy.

Daisy tiptoed through the east wing into the hyphen that connected it with the main block of the house. She passed the closed door to the basement and continued walking, glancing into the dining room, salon, and parlor as she walked by. Nothing seemed to be disturbed. When she got to the grand staircase in the west wing, she called out and thought she heard a noise from below.

She called out again, but got no answer and had just decided to check the cellar when she heard Sammy Davis, Jr. singing that he really needed to be himself from above. "Dad, is that you?"

She jumped when Len Rutherford said, "Daisy?" as he slowly came down the staircase. Daisy said, "Sorry, you startled me. You have the same ringtone that my dad has."

"Do I? I've been searching for your mother and Ms. Long. They got away from me when I was on the phone with you. Are you alone?" as he came down the stairs.

"Yes. Rose was out when you called and you made it sound so urgent I just ran out of the house."

"You didn't bring that dog with you, did you?"

"Malcolm? Why would I? I know you don't care for dogs and it was raining."

"Sorry. I know it's silly, but dogs do give me a scare."

"That's all right. I don't think he'd be offended. In fact, he might take it as a compliment. Anyway, where have you looked? I called when I got here, but no one answered."

Len said, "I was checking upstairs. I haven't looked in the basement, yet. I wish those two had waited for me. You don't think they'd be wandering around outside in all the rain."

He looked at Daisy standing at the bottom of the stairs. "I remember seeing you standing right there on the day Wally died. You had a blue dress on. It suited you."

"Oh, thank you. I liked it."

"Did the paint come out? I noticed it on your dress and hoped it wouldn't be ruined."

She looked at him oddly. "No. Unfortunately, it's a goner. It was one of my favorites, too." She felt in her pocket for the heavy flashlight and gripped it tightly. "Anyway, as to wandering around in the rain, you never know what my mother will do. We should probably check outside."

"I think we'd better have a quick look in the basement first."

Daisy hesitated. "Sure. I guess that makes sense." She led the way back to the servants' staircase in the east wing of the house praying that the dogs would stay put and keep quiet. When they got to the basement door Len said, "Ladies first."

"The lights aren't on. I doubt they're down there. Maybe we should call the police again."

"I don't think we need the police, Daisy. It's not an emergency. We'll manage without them just fine."

She paused in the doorway. "Len, how did you know that was paint on my dress?"

He shook his head and pulled something from his pocket. "Me and my big mouth. Mentioning that was a mistake, wasn't it?" She saw a glint of metal in his hand and tried to back away. He ran his hand through his hair and sighed. His voice was sad, yet somehow menacing as he said, "Just get down the stairs, please. I really don't want to hurt you, Daisy."

He grabbed her arm and shoved her forward. She caught herself on the door frame in time to keep from tumbling down the steep flight of steps. He hissed, "Daisy, do you want me to hit you again? Just get going!"

"I can't see."

"You know the layout. You'll be fine."

She managed to grope her way down without falling.

At the bottom she switched on the wall lamp. Shadows sprang up around the room in the dim light. As her eyes adjusted she thought she could make out what looked like a body lying on the far side of the work room.

"Len, what have you done?" She started toward it, but he grabbed her again and she felt the point of the knife at her neck. He forced her toward the wine cellar. Daisy whispered, "Len, what's going on? Who is that?"

"Leo Walters."

"Where is my mother? Is she all right?"

"She's fine. The old bags are both fine. Turn on the lamp."

At the doorway of the wine cellar Daisy felt for the other wall lamp and turned it on. She could see her mother and Adele in the corner. At first glance she thought they were just huddled together, but then she saw the ropes and the tape on their mouths.

Len Rutherford said, "Now, we're going to find my silver and then I'll get out of here."

He pushed Daisy into the room. "Take the tape off them. The old lady's going to talk one way or another."

Daisy carefully pulled the tape from her mother's and Adele's mouths. "Are you okay? Did he hurt you? What happened?"

Angela said, "I'm all right." She sat up straight and rubbed her wrists. "When I got to Adele's house, I found her lying on the floor. I was trying to help her up when the sniveling coward snuck up on me. He trussed us up and marched us up here." Angela glared at Len Rutherford. "Daisy, that animal hit her again and again. And I'm afraid he might have killed Leo when he came looking for us."

Daisy took Adele's arm and said, "Adele, can you hear me?"

Adele leaned heavily against Angela and tried to open her eyes. "Where is Leo?"

Daisy turned to Len Rutherford and hollered, "What kind of person does this - beats up an old lady?"

"If she hadn't lied to me, I wouldn't have hit her. All I want is what's mine."

"What's yours? What the hell are you talking about?"

Adele whispered, "The Revere silver. He wants the Revere silver."

"It belongs to me. It's my inheritance." He glowered at Adele. "You and your precious family. You threw Matilda out and took her dowry. Well, I'm taking it back!"

"Matilda? She's been dead for two hundred years. What's Matilda got to do with any of this?" asked Daisy.

"She was my grandmother. That's my right. My family never forgot the way she was treated. Her brother threw her out and left her penniless. Threw her away like so much garbage just because she fell in love with the wrong man."

"Len, that's history. Times were different and you can't possibly know everything that happened."

"She wrote it all down in her diary. I found it when my father died. The whole disgusting story is in there. The only person who was kind to her was her sister Amelia. Her letters were with the diary. Amelia told her about the tunnels and the silver. And how her beloved brother gave her a little of the silver for her dowry and kept the rest hidden for himself."

"That's the diary I found under the sofa, isn't it?"

Len's voice softened. "I'm really sorry about that. My mistake. I should have hidden it in a better place. I had with me early that day hoping to find the stash. There were maps of the house in it, as well as the tunnels. When I couldn't find the silver hidden underground, I figured it must still be in the house. I was going to search under the floorboards.

"But people started coming in early to set up. I

shoved it under the cushion where you found it. I didn't want to hit you, Daisy, but I couldn't let you read it. I hated hurting you. I'm very fond of you, you know that." He smiled. "If the old bag would just give up the silver, we could go away together. It's worth millions. We could buy an island or something and never have to look back."

Daisy didn't know whether to laugh or cry. Even if he weren't a murderer the idea that they would run off together was ludicrous. She stepped forward, putting herself between Len and the two older women. "I don't think that would work. I have a life here. My family, my business. I couldn't leave."

"You could. If you cared enough about me, you could."

Daisy moved slowly toward him, her hand grasping the Maglite in her pocket. "Len, of course I care about you, but we need time to get to know each other."

He looked at her, then laughed. "I know what you're doing. You think I'll fall for this, this act. You think you can keep me here until help comes, don't you?"

"Not really. But I do have a question. Why would you think the silver was still hidden after all these years?"

"Because it has never been found. The family knew where it was. They must have. But sweet Aunt Adele says there isn't any silver. She's lying. It's still hidden. She just doesn't want a Rutherford to have it."

Daisy softened her voice and asked, "Len, would Adele really have sold her home if she had that kind of money at her disposal? Think about it." She took a step back and waved her hand. "There's nothing here."

"There is. And I'll find it."

Len was right about one thing. Daisy did want to keep him talking until Rose got there. She hesitated, then asked, "Len, why did you kill Wally Stone?"

"He found the tunnel, like you did, and was going to

call the cops. He thought he could outsmart me. He couldn't."

"And Leo?"

"Leo! That wimp was nosing around trying to play hero pretending to protect this place. He must know where the silver is hidden and just didn't want me to find it."

Adele tried to speak, but the words were barely audible. "I've tried to tell you, there isn't any silver. It's all gone."

Suddenly, he grabbed Daisy by the shoulders and shoved her hard against the wall in back of him. He held the knife close to her face and said, "I don't believe you. Now, old lady, you're going to tell me where my sweet old great-grandma hid that treasure."

Daisy's heart was racing, but spoke quietly. "Leo, please don't do this." Just then there was a loud crash from upstairs that sounded to Daisy a lot like two small dogs slamming a door against a wall. He shouted at Daisy. "You said you were alone."

"I was, but I told Rose to call the police before I left. We thought we were looking for Leo."

Len looked around the cellar and came to a decision. He said, "You're coming with me."

"I'm what?"

"We're going out through the tunnel and I'm keeping you until I get what's mine."

He jerked Daisy's left arm behind her, and employed his knife again. "Ow! That hurts."

"Just until I can get you out of here." He pulled her out of the wine cellar and under the archway toward the back of the storeroom.

She yelled at him, "You are stark raving crackers. Did you know that?" He pulled harder on her arm and she shrieked.

They had reached the entrance to the tunnel and

Rutherford had just opened the hatch when a fury of fur came flying through the room. Malcolm leaped up and sunk his teeth into the arm holding the knife. Len Rutherford let out a howl of terrified rage and the knife clattered to the ground.

Daisy broke free and managed to pull her flashlight out of her pocket. She swung for all she was worth aiming at his head, but he ducked and she got his shoulder. Malcolm bared his teeth ready to attack again, but Rutherford screamed at the little dog, jumped into the hole and started running like a crazy man.

Malcolm leaped in after him and landed badly, but he got up and started after him. Daisy shouted, "No, Malcolm. Stay here. Let him go. He won't get far now that we know who he is." She carefully dropped into the hole and picked up the little mutt. "Rats. I just wish we had time to get to the outside end. We could have locked him in."

She righted the ladder and hoisted Malcolm into the storeroom. As she started to pull herself up she heard footsteps running back toward her. All at once she was standing in a bank of fog. It came up the tunnel, rolled passed her and out into the storeroom, filled the basement, then seemed to escape through the casement window.

Daisy stood still. Rutherford had stopped a few yards away. She saw sheer terror on his face as he looked up to see Malcolm, and now Percy, snarling at the top of the entrance. He turned back toward the darkness and let out a blood curdling scream. Then he sank to his knees and curled into a ball.

Daisy looked into the gloom of the tunnel and saw Sophia Long wreathed in shimmering mist standing guard. Daisy nodded to her, quickly climbed out of the tunnel, closed the hatch, and pulled a heavy chest over it.

Chapter Twenty-Two

Daisy could hear Len Rutherford screaming incoherently. She untied Angela and left her to free Adele while she went over to check Leo. She felt his pulse and shouted, "He's breathing."

Footsteps sounded in the hall above them. Rose opened the door and called, "Daisy?"

"Rose? Down here. Hurry, we need a doctor."

Rose dialed 911 as she clattered down the stairs. "I'm calling for an ambulance now, and Brian's on his way." She gave them the address, then screamed, "Please hurry!" when she saw Daisy bending over Leo's body. "Oh my God, is it Mother?"

Daisy looked up from Leo and said, "No, Mother's all right. But Adele is badly hurt and Leo's unconscious."

Angela came to the doorway of the wine cellar and said, "Rose, help me with Adele."

Rose found Adele struggling to get up. Her left eye was swollen shut and turning blue. She had nasty bruises around her neck and was in obvious pain, but she said, "Take me to Leo. He was so brave. If that man killed him, I don't know what I'll do."

They helped Adele over to Leo. She knelt beside him and held his hand. Daisy said, "I think he'll be all right, Adele. He's breathing and his pulse is good. Mother, you don't have your smelling salts with you by any chance, do you?"

Rose pulled a little vial out of her shoulder bag. "I do. Mother trained me well. Like a model Girl Scout, I'm always prepared." She opened it and waved it under Leo's nose. To Adele's great relief, he opened his eyes and moaned, gripped his aunt's hand briefly, and closed his eyes again.

Angela made a pillow out of her jacket for Leo and Daisy found a chair for Adele. Then they waited in an exhausted silence for help to come.

Suddenly Rose asked, "Who is that screaming?"

Daisy said, "Len Rutherford. He's in the tunnel."

"Well, why doesn't he just go out the other end?"

"Sophia's standing guard. I'm not sure who scares him more, the dogs or the ghost."

Early the next morning Daisy, Rose and Angela were sitting in the living room of The Elms sipping mimosas with Roscoe, Malcolm, and Percy snoring gently in their laps. Peter came in from the kitchen and held up the pitcher. "Anyone need a refill? Or maybe just coffee or tea?"

Daisy held her glass out. "Why not? We're not opening the shop today and I'm going to need something to help me sleep."

"And I think just a tad more would be lovely." Angela stroked Percy's bandaged head and said, "You are a brave boy. What a night!" She looked at her daughters and smiled. "At least your father didn't show up."

Daisy said, "Yes, that would certainly have been the icing on the meatloaf. I wonder where he is."

"He left me a little note. He's gone to Boston to see an attorney. Something about Lydia's estate."

"Well, he'll be sorry he missed it, won't he? He does love a bit of excitement and he could have seen Sophia for himself."

"Only if he got in the tunnel with that madman. I didn't get to see her. What was she wearing?" Rose asked.

"Same thing as before, I think. I'm not sure how extensive a ghost's wardrobe would be. Anyway, I didn't get a really good look. The light was bad and Len was moaning. All in all, I didn't think it was the best time for a chat." She stopped talking, cocked her ear and said, "Do I hear teeth grinding?"

"That would be me. Anybody want to tell me what the hell has been going on?" Brian Hathaway stood in front of the fireplace. The look on his face clearly said that he was not amused.

"Ah! I was going to tell you everything on our date tonight," Daisy said. "But I guess now would be better, huh?"

"Yes. Now would be the perfect time."

Brian had gotten to the mansion just after the ambulance. Before he got there, Daisy and Rose had run out to the woods and jammed a couple of fallen branches against the opening in the ice house to keep Len in, just in case Sophia's presence wasn't enough.

By the time the police got him out he was almost incoherent with fear. He kept repeating, "She's sending me to the dogs. They'll eat me alive."

Daisy, Rose and Angela had followed the ambulance to the emergency room and spent the rest of the night with Adele and Leo, not leaving until they were assured that both were out of danger. They had come home to find Peter fixing coffee for a less than happy Brian Hathaway.

He looked at Daisy and said, "Any time. I'm listening."

"All right. I'll begin at the beginning, but hear me out before you go ballistic." She told him about finding the paint in the basement, the scrap of a map outside, the tunnels, Leo's orange cloth, and the diary. "We figured that if we knew where the tunnels were before I told you, it would save you a lot of trouble. And you were so busy this week with the world seeming to fall apart, I didn't want to drop another load on you. And, besides, you had all the same clues that we did - well, almost all."

During the recitation, Brian had gone through a variety of rather comical facial expressions. However, the main one seemed to be a stoic sort of acceptance. "I could arrest all of you for obstruction."

Daisy smiled. "But you won't, will you?"

"No. I won't. Too much paper work and I did catch Stone's killer."

"Sit down, have a mimosa. You deserve a little time off," said Daisy.

Peter handed Brian a glass and said, "Just go with the flow. It's easier." Peter then dropped into a chair with his own drink and said, "I have quite a few questions about this whole thing myself."

Angela got up and said, "Well, I'm sure they will all be answered, but first we are going to have a proper breakfast. I feel the need of something comforting."

Angela wouldn't allow another word spoken about the affair until they had finished the Eggs Benedict that she whipped up to go with grapefruit and tea.

Daisy and Rose were cleaning up in the kitchen when Daisy remembered the mess she had left when she hurried out. "Who do I thank for cleaning up the floor?"

Peter answered, "Me. What was that stuff anyway?"

"Some sort of smoothie that Len Rutherford brought over for me. It was too gross looking to drink, so I stuck it in the frig. It fell out when I was rushing to leave and I just left it there."

"He gave you a smoothie?" asked Brian.

"Yes. He brought it by when we were out. He told me it was good for a quick recovery after I got hit on the head." She stopped putting dishes in the washer and slammed the door. "Actually, after HE hit me on the head. That weirdo scumbag!"

Brian looked at Peter. "What did you do with the rag you used to clean it up?"

"Paper towels – in the trash." Brian pulled the bag out of the bin, glanced in, then sealed it with tape and initialed it.

Daisy asked, "Why? What's my smoothie got to...?" She gasped. "It was the same stuff that was in the cellar near Wally's body. The stuff I stepped in! Dammit, I should have realized it when it spilled. I would have known it was Len, not Leo, we were looking for."

"And, of course, then you would never have gone up there alone."

"Of course not. I'd have waited for Rose."

Finally, they were all seated in the dining room. Brian smacked the table and said, "Okay. Breakfast eaten, dishes done. Let's talk."

Angela asked, "Will this be the official police statement or are we just chatting?"

Brian glanced at her. "What difference would that make? I assume the story isn't going to change."

"Well, of course not. But I will need to watch my language if this is being recorded for the police. I don't normally use profanity, but in the case of that son of a sea cook, I might."

Brian smiled. "For right now, just tell me what happened last night."

They sat there looking at each other. Angela sighed. "Well, I guess I'll start. I have been concerned about Adele for quite a while. We all have. She's been more scatty than usual and I had the feeling she was hiding something and I was sure it had to do with the problems at the mansion. It took some coaxing, but she finally confided in me that she thought Leo might be in trouble.'

Daisy said, "Mother, you should have told us."

"Adele wasn't positive what he was doing and didn't want anyone to know. I promised her I'd keep it to myself until we found out what was going on.

"She called last night in a state. She couldn't get hold of Leo and was afraid something had happened to him. I know Adele seems like a tough old bird, but Leo is all she has. So I went over to the Dower House."

Angela stopped talking and took a deep breath. She sat up very straight, placed her fingertips on her clavicle, and closed her eyes. Brian said, "What is she doing?"

Rose answered, "She's centering herself. It's a wonderful device for calming the nerves."

Angela opened her eyes and continued, "I got to Adele's home and found the door open. I stepped in and saw Adele lying in the doorway to the dining room. I thought she had fallen, but when I got to her I saw that her face had been badly bruised. Then suddenly, someone grabbed my arm and twisted it behind me. I couldn't see who it was, but I could hear Percy growling. There was a scream and I was practically tossed onto the dining room table. That's when I saw Len Rutherford hit Percy with a candlestick. My poor little guy just lay there. I thought he was dead."

Rose held her mother's hand and Percy jumped into her lap. "I got up, but he had grabbed Adele and was holding a knife to her throat. He said he'd kill her if I didn't do as he said.

"He marched us up the driveway to the mansion and on into the cellar." Tears sprang to her eyes and she looked away for a moment. "There was nothing I could do to stop him. I was afraid he'd kill her if I tried anything."

Peter quietly got up and poured a little bourbon into Angela's teacup. She said, "He shoved us into the corner of the wine cellar and tied us up. Then he started interrogating Adele, asking her about the silver over and over. She kept telling him that there was no silver, that it was gone, he didn't believe her. One time he hit her so hard that she lost consciousness for a moment."

Angela sipped her tea and sighed. Brian said, "Take your time."

"I told him that killing Adele wouldn't help him find the silver. He said maybe I was right. That's when he called Daisy. I have no idea why."

"How did Leo get into the picture?" asked Daisy.

"Oh poor Leo. Apparently, Leo's been more or less guarding the place. Adele was so worried about the way he's been acting that she confronted him this afternoon – well, yesterday afternoon.

"And he confessed to what he was doing. He told her he hadn't wanted to frighten her, but that he knew someone had found the way into the mansion through the tunnels. He's been roaming around the grounds, walking through the tunnels, trying to find out who was using them."

Daisy got up and paced around the table. "Well, I wish I'd known. We all could have kept a look out."

Brian shook his head. "Does it occur to any of you to call the police? Ever?"

"Of course, it does." Daisy patted his back. "You're here, aren't you?"

Angela went on. "I suppose Leo must have seen Rutherford taking us into the mansion and decided to sneak in by the tunnel entrance.

"But Rutherford must have heard him in the tunnel. He taped our mouths, grabbed one of the wine bottles, and left us bundled in the corner. I heard the trap door open. Then a sickening thud, then another. That monster walked back into the wine cellar, looked me right in the eye, laughed, and said, 'Kind of how I got Wally! Only I got Wally with an iron, but the bottle worked pretty well.'"

Rose said, "Lord love a duck, the guy is insane."

"I'm sure that will be his defense," added Brian.

Daisy looked puzzled. "Why was he upstairs when I got there?"

Angela shrugged. "That was the oddest thing about the whole appalling business. After he attacked Leo he looked at his watch and said, 'Daisy should be here soon. I'd better get upstairs to meet her. You two stay here,' as if all this were perfectly normal."

Everyone was silent for a long time. Brian took Angela's hand and said, "I'm sorry this happened to you."

His cell rang and he took the call in the other room. When he came back he said, "Mr. Rutherford seems to be in a talking mood. I'm going to have to leave."

Rose piped up. "Well, you can read this before you talk to him." She handed Brian a folder. "It's Len Rutherford's family history. My friend, Sally, did some investigating for me and it seems that our Len Rutherford – whose name is actually Leonard Long Rutherford…"

Daisy practically jumped out of her chair. "I knew it was a lion, but it was Leonard the Lion, not Leo. Why didn't I think of that earlier?"

Rose continued, "Anyway, his name aside, he may think he's a relative and entitled to a large portion of that silver wherever it may be, but Sally traced his line back and he simply is not. Slant it any way he'd like, he's just a random cousin in the Rutherford line, not the Longs."

Brian flipped through the file and said, "Thanks, Rose. Ladies, I'll be in touch."

Daisy walked him to the door. "Are you absolutely furious with us, well, me?"

"Not absolutely." He kissed her forehead. "Daisy, you could have been killed."

"But I wasn't and we caught the bad guy. And now you get to go listen to what he has to say. And if he tells you he saw Sophia, he isn't insane. She was most definitely there!"

Chapter Twenty-Three

The weather at Halloween in the Washington DC area can range from literally freezing where the witches and princesses are all but buried under coats, scarves and gloves to a fairly mild night where a heavy shirt under that Batman costume fills the bill.

But once in a great while, and this year was one of those, the area is treated to an unexpected bonus - a spectacular Indian summer. Afternoons of warm sunshine and balmy evenings. Daisy and Rose decided to move the party outside. The shop was closed until Monday and they spent the morning hanging lights outside and decorating the sunroom and porch.

Daisy and Malcolm were putting the finishing touches on his house - cobwebs, spiders, and bats - and Rose was on a ladder hanging a ghostly piñata in the oak tree when Angela came by with Adele.

"Adele, how are you? Come inside and sit down. You look exhausted."

"Thank you, dear. I think I will." Adele was wearing a scarlet boa over her bright blue caftan that covered the bruises on her neck, but Daisy gasped when she saw the purplish/black bruises on her face.

Rose said, "Shouldn't you be in the hospital?"

"They sent me home. It all looks worse than it is."

Angela laughed. "They sent you home! You got up and said you were leaving. That's when they sent you home. I spoke to the doctor and Adele is right. Nothing broken, thank God, and really she just needs rest and time."

"That's wonderful news. How is Leo?"

Adele smiled happily. "He's all right and should be home tomorrow. He has a severe concussion and they want to watch him and run some tests. His head still aches, but he was walking and talking this morning. We Longs are a tough bunch."

"You are indeed, but even so, I would think you ought to be home resting."

"I will be. Your mother has kindly volunteered to be my chauffer today and I wanted to come here and thank you for all you did. We might have died without you and Rose."

"Well, you should be thanking Sophia and the dogs," said Daisy. "They were the ones who really caught him. What can I get you? I can make a pot of tea or we have pitcher of Spooky Juice ready to go, if it's not too early."

"I think I'd like to try a bit of that." Rose handed her a small glass of the purple liquid. "It looks quite, well, spooky!"

"Nothing for me, dear," said Angela. "I've got a lot to do this afternoon and, of course, I'm driving."

They sat for a few minutes enjoying the day when Rose finally said, "All right. I've waited long enough to ask. Where is the Revere treasure?"

Adele put her glass down and said, "There isn't any."

"But didn't I use a Revere spoon to stir my tea?"

"You did. And that's the extent of the treasure."

Daisy asked, "Are you sure? Nothing's hidden in those tunnels?"

"Of course not. The Revere pieces were never hidden in the tunnel."

"But isn't that what Matilda's diary said?"

"I haven't read that diary. But I have read Amelia's. Strange, she only mentions Matilda once or twice. I didn't know they corresponded. Perhaps she was afraid Ambrose might find out. At any rate, according to Amelia, Sophia Long was going to bury the silver, but decided to entrust it to a dear friend instead. After her death this friend contacted Ambrose. His father was still alive and so they kept the silver hidden."

Angela looked puzzled. "Why wasn't it used for the girls' dowries as Sophia intended?"

"Ah. First, only Amelia required one. Matilda was outcast and poor little Louise died when she was just fifteen, so he was able to apportion a much larger property to Amelia. Secondly, when Josiah died not long after Sophia his debts were considerable and little actual cash was left, so Ambrose held onto the silver.

"And through all these years that the family has owned Holly Hill, it has come in handy. A little here, a little there, sold off quietly to keep the place running. The depression took the last of it, except for the one teaspoon. We kept it as a token of Sophia."

Daisy shook her head. "Wally was killed for a treasure that no longer exists. Does Brian know all of this?"

"Oh yes. He and I spent quite a while together yesterday. That Detective Hathaway is a very nice man, Daisy."

Rose got up and looked out into the garden at the sun shining brightly on the scarlet chrysanthemums. She turned and said, "One other thing I've been wondering about. Well, two actually. Do you think Dad had anything to do with all of this?"

"Your father may be many things, but basically he's a lazy so-and-so. He wouldn't bother going after some doubtful treasure. Too much work. Much more likely he'd try to con Rutherford out of it after he'd done the heavy lifting. I think, maybe, Len Rutherford thought he could use Dickie in some way, though I'm not sure how."

Daisy said, "I think you've hit the nail on the head, Mom."

"Then that brings me to my next question, the one we've all been asking since he got here – what is our darling father up to?"

"Maybe we'll find out at the party tonight," answered Daisy.

Adele got to her feet with some difficulty. "Well, Angela, if you don't mind I rather think I would like to go home and rest. Have a lovely party, girls. You certainly have the weather for it and these little drinks should keep it quite lively."

Brian Hathaway, rather dashing in his deerstalker hat, took a contemplative puff on his meerschaum pipe. He smiled as he watched Daisy, the Bavarian barmaid, pass a tray of hors d'oeuvres to her guests.

Tray empty, she sat beside him on the porch swing and said, "You came! I was afraid you might still be angry with me."

He laughed. "I figured the best way to keep you out of trouble is to stick close to you."

"Well, I'm glad you're here. And in costume! I didn't think you'd have time. You make a pretty good Sherlock Holmes."

"I've got to say you make quite a lovely barmaid."

"Danke." She got up, curtsied, and did a little twirl. "I'd better check on things in the kitchen. I left Rose mixing the punch, but I think she was sipping more than she was pouring. Would you like to help?"

"Sure."

Just then a voice boomed, "I'm late, I'm late for a very important date!" Dickie Forrest was standing at the gate looking at his pocket watch.

Daisy said, "Well, if it's not the Mad Hatter. Dad, 'I

shall be too late' is the White Rabbit's line."

"Is it? Who knew?"

"Everybody. Come on in and make yourself at home – as if you ever did anything else."

Annie Oakley and Buffalo Bill, aka Rose and Peter, came out of the sunroom carrying a large pitcher of Spooky Juice which she deposited on the bar. Rose called out, "Let's get this party started!"

It was almost nine when Dickie came over to Rose as she was lighting coals in the fire pit. "Isn't your mother coming? I need to talk to her."

"Mother's coming. But please don't make a scene tonight. The party's going so nicely. Don't spoil it."

"When have I ever? I just want to make sure she's all right. She's been through a terrible nightmare and I wasn't here to help her. You could have knocked me over with a feather when I heard about Len. He seemed like such a nice guy."

"Well, he's not. And you can thank your lucky stars that he told Brian that you had nothing to do with any of the business at the mansion. You were definitely looking suspicious. I kept hearing that stupid ringtone of yours, but it turns out you're not the only nut who has 'got to be you'."

"He must have copied it from me. Now I'll have to change it. What would be good?"

"*You're So Vain*?"

Dickie laughed. "Rose, you know me too well. I might go with *Rocky*!"

"You go, Dad."

At nine-thirty a vision walked through the doors of the sunroom and onto the porch. Daisy burst out laughing. Rose said, "I love it!"

Marilyn Monroe in her iconic white halter dress was escorted in by a diminutive Mickey Mantle, bat in hand proudly wearing his Yankees pinstripes. Dot and

Angela beamed. Angela said, "I think Dot makes a lovely Marilyn, don't you?"

"That she does." Peter eyed the baseball bat. "Are you planning on hitting one out this evening?"

"You never know."

By one o'clock the crowd had thinned leaving only Angela, Dickie, Daisy, and Rose.

They sat around the fire pit looking up at the stars. Dickie sighed and put his arm around Angela. "Isn't this nice? Just the way it used to be. Me and my girls together again."

Angela removed his arm and said, "No more Spooky Juice for you. It's clearly gone to your head and it's time for you to go."

"But Angie, I need to talk to you."

"Not tonight, you don't. Dickie, you don't seem to be getting the message. I've forgiven you. And I can almost say that I've forgotten, although I'm not quite there. But I don't love you and we are not getting back together."

"I don't think you mean that. I think we should consult the Ouija board again."

"Dickie, as much as I love a good séance, I do realize that no one is going to contact you through the Ouija. Certainly not Lydia. She's probably floating around somewhere, knocking back the odd Tequila Sunrise and thoroughly enjoying herself. Why would she want to bother with us?"

"Please, Angie. Just once more. I've got the feeling that she really wants to tell us something."

Daisy said, "Dad, it's late. Go home. Maybe we'll play one day this week."

He got up and stretched. "It's a date. Thursday."

Rose started collecting glasses. "Okay. Ouija. One last time before I throw the stupid thing out!"

Smiling broadly Dickie doffed his hat and said, "I'll

bring the wine."

Angela watched him go and said, "What does that man really want?"

Thursday morning, Rose sipped her English Breakfast as she read the story Maisie Bailey had written about the murder in the Bostwick Bulletin. "She writes very well. And her editor let her keep the ghost angle. She made it sound very mysterious!"

Sha handed Daisy the paper. "Nice picture of Adele and Leo."

Daisy looked at the large picture above the fold - Adele and Leo, looking a little worse for the wear, standing in front of Holly Hill Mansion. She started to read the article, but stopped and took the paper over to the window so she could see it in the bright sunlight. "What's that?"

Rose got up and looked over her shoulder. "What?"

Daisy pointed to a shadow in the window of the hall. "That!"

Rose said, "That's a smudge."

"It is not a smudge."

Rose looked a little closer, then got out a magnifying glass and examined the picture. She drew in her breath and muttered, "Holy catfish!" She handed Daisy the magnifier.

"I don't need it. I already know. It's Sophia. She's still keeping watch."

Roscoe sat on the top of the china closet and watched Dick Forrest set up the Ouija board on the dining room table. He lit candles and incense, hung a small wind chime from the wall sconce, and opened a bottle of champagne.

Rose walked in from the kitchen and said, "Dad, is all this necessary? You know this thing doesn't really talk to you. What do you think you're going to prove? And what's with the champagne?"

"We're going to be celebrating. I'm proving to your mother that I want her back. That we can start again. She is coming, isn't she?"

Rose shook her head. "Yes. She said she'd be here. I'm not sure she'll want to fool around with the Ouija though. You know Dad, I have not the foggiest notion of why, after all these years, you have chosen to start this nonsense, but I can tell you that it's a lost cause."

"We'll see. I think Lydia will convince her."

"Okay. I give up."

Rose heard Frank Sinatra singing *I Did It My Way* and Dickie pulled his cell phone out and said, "I'll take this in the hall." A few minutes later he came back in.

"No *Rocky Theme*?" asked Rose.

"No, I thought I'd stick with Rat Pack. Where's your sister?"

"In the shop closing up."

Daisy and Angela came up the stairs together. Percy was right behind them. He was still sporting a bandage on his little head and wearing a cone collar. He didn't look happy with the whole state of affairs. Malcolm toddled over to him and tugged at the cone as Percy whined and tried to scratch it off.

Angela said, "All right. But do not scratch your head."

She took the collar off and Percy and Malcolm headed down the back stairs to the dog door. "The vet says he's fine, and doesn't need the collar or the bandage, but he looks so cute I keep putting them on him."

She looked around the room and beamed. "Perfect!" Angela took off her coat and draped it over an armchair. She was wearing her monk's robe underneath and pulled the cowl over her head. "Well, Dickie, I've got the feeling that we really will learn something tonight. Let's do this."

Daisy and Rose looked at each other. Daisy whispered, "What's going on? Yesterday she said you couldn't pay her to play this with Dad again." Rose shrugged and shook her head.

They turned off the lights and settled around the table. Angela said, "Tonight just Dickie and I will be using the pointer. You don't mind, do you, girls?"

Rose said, "Nope. Whatever floats your boat. We'll watch." She poured herself a glass of bubbly and sat back. Roscoe jumped onto Daisy's lap and stared at the board.

Dickie and Angela placed their fingertips on the pointer. Angela said, "Why don't you lead the chant, Dickie."

He looked hopeful. "I think you're right, Angie. This is going to be a big night. I can feel it. I think Lydia is already here." He closed his eyes. "Ouija, Ouija are you there?"

There was no movement. Angela said, "Try again. I feel a presence in the room, too. I'm sure some someone will answer."

Dickie looked uncertain. "Angie, I mean Angela, are you all right."

"Of course I'm all right. Why do you ask?"

"Well, I got the feeling the other night that you're just doing this to get me out of your hair. But now you seem, I don't know, different."

"I feel strongly that we will learn something of interest to us both very shortly. Go on, Dickie, ask again."

Dickie intoned, "Ouija, Ouija, are you there?"

This time the pointer moved slowly to YES.

He said, "We are here to speak to Lydia Forrest. May we speak to Lydia? Lydia Forrest are you there? Can you hear us?"

This time the pointer spelled out I AM HERE.

Dickie looked excited. He said, "I can't believe this. Are you moving the pointer, Angie? Because I'm not."

"Were you ever?"

He looked confused. "Oh. Of course, not."

"Well, I wouldn't either. I told you I feel a presence."

"This is great." He lowered his voice. "Lydia, it's me, your nephew, Dickie. I'm here with my wife, Angela."

Angela cooed, "Please, Dickie darling. Ex-wife."

"Sorry. Lydia, we're here. Dickie and Angela. The last time we spoke, I was sure you were trying to tell us something. What do you want to tell us?" The pointer didn't move, but the prisms hanging in the window began to tinkle. Dickie started a little and looked around the room.

Daisy rolled her eyes. "It's the heat coming on."

Dickie laughed uncomfortably.

Angela said, "Perhaps you're asking the wrong question. Let me try. Lydia, dear, is there something you would like me to do for you?"

YES

"What would that be?"

R E A D T H E L E T T E R

Dickie said, "What does that mean? Read the letter?"

"I think she's referring to this." Angela got up from the table, turned on the light, and opened her purse. She pulled a large envelope out. "A letter to me from Crane, Poole and Schmidt, Lydia's attorneys."

Dickie jumped out of his chair. "You were moving that pointer, weren't you?"

"Of course I was. Do you think I'm an idiot?"

Rose asked, "What am I missing here?"

"Your father wanted to use Lydia to get me back in order to get his grubby little hands on her estate. This is a letter from her lawyers. In it they tell me that Marie and I are Lydia's only beneficiaries. Marie gets the house. I get the rest."

"Dad! All this for a couple of bucks?"

Dickie turned bright red. "Not a couple of bucks, Lydia was loaded. And, well, it wasn't just the money. I'm getting older and I need someone to take care of me."

"Well, the joke's on you pal," laughed Angela. "There is no money. She gave it all to charity before she died. I get the family jewelry to pass on to our girls. The value isn't tremendous, but the sentiment is."

"No money?"

"No, you ass. All your shenanigans were for nothing." She stared at Dickie, then sighed. "You gave me my beautiful daughters. So, if you are ever truly alone and in need, I'll find you a suitable home. As for taking care of you in your dotage, in your dreams, you old fool."

Rose poured champagne for everyone. Dickie raised his glass. "It was worth a try. To you Angela. You were always my favorite gal."

Malcolm and Percy came into the room just as Dickie was leaving. Daisy said, "Well, that explains a lot."

Rose said, "What a piece of work! Are you all right, Mother?"

Angela looked thoughtful. "Yes, I'm fine. I certainly didn't want him back. But I would like to have believed he was actually sorry. Oh well, you can't have everything and I've got so much more than most." She smiled at her girls and picked Percy up. "Don't I, sweetie?"

They looked out the window and watched as Dick Forrest stood on the sidewalk and pulled out his phone. A moment later his red Mustang pulled up in front. A tall, slender brunette in her early fifties got out, gave

Dickie a hug, handed him the keys and they both got in. Angela watched them drive away. "His favorite gal, my eye!" She drained her wineglass in one gulp. "Anyone for a refill?"

THE END

Author Bio

Penny Clover Petersen grew up in the Washington DC area with her brother and four sisters.

Penny lives with her husband Tom in Bowie, Maryland. As a stay-at-home mother she also held a series of part-time jobs while raising their children.

When she's not writing, she enjoys time with her children, grandchildren and large extended family. She likes to travel, refurbish old furniture, and collect family stories and recipes for the 'family cookbook.

She loves historic homes and is a docent at Riversdale Mansion in Riverdale, MD.

ROSE'S COCKTAIL HOUR

SPOOKY JUICE
Absolutely the only thing to serve when a ghost drops by
1 oz. Vodka
½ oz. Blue Curaçao liqueur
½ oz. Triple Sec
1 dash grenadine
Shake with ice. Strain and serve in martini glass.

BASEBALL PLEASURE
A lovely cocktail suitable for funerals and other sporting
events In a highball glass filled with ice mix:
2 oz. Vodka
4 oz. orange juice

Add:
1 jigger Whiskey
1 jigger Amaretto
Mix well.
Garnish with a little pennant supporting your favorite team
or loved one.

TROUBLE NAMED FATHER
He's back and he wasn't invited!
1½ oz. Brandy
½ oz. Apricot Brandy
2 T. cranberry juice cocktail
Shake with ice. Strain into cocktail glass.

BEE'S KNEES
The perfect lubrication when planning a séance
2 oz. dry Gin
¾ oz. honey syrup*
½ oz. fresh lemon juice
Shake with ice and strain into chilled martini glass.
Garnish with lemon twist.
*Honey Syrup
1 cup honey
1 cup very hot water
Stir until honey is dissolved.
Cool before using.
Refrigerate in an airtight container for up to several weeks.

SÉANCE SURPRISE
Ouija, Ouija are you there?
1½ oz. Vodka
1½ oz. Banana Liqueur
Shake with ice. Strain into cocktail glass.

SLY SPY
When you want to know just what your ex is up to
1½ oz. Vodka
2 oz. orange juice
2 oz. cranberry juice
Pour into a highball glass, stir, and fill with ice.

KENTUCKY CORPSE REVIVER
Séance anyone?
¾ oz. Bourbon
¾ oz. Curacao
¾ oz. freshly-squeezed lemon juice
¾ oz. Lillet Blanc or Blonde Dubonnet
Mint Spring
Shake with ice and strain into chilled bowl-shaped wine glass and garnish with mint.

BABBLING IDIOT
When you really need to stop saying dumb things, try this. They won't sound nearly so stupid!
1½ cups cranberries, fresh or frozen
1 cup cranberry juice cocktail
⅔ cup sugar
Juice and zest of 1 orange
750 ml. Prosecco or any nice sparkling wine, very cold
Blend cranberries and cranberry juice in a food processor until berries are roughly chopped.
Combine berry mixture, sugar, orange juice and zest in a saucepan.
Bring to boil and simmer 10 minutes.
Cool at room temperature.
Just before serving, place 1 T. of syrup in each champagne glass and add wine.

SOPHIA'S GHOST

A little something for your very first ghost sighting

1½ oz. Tequila
1½ oz. orange juice
2 dashes grenadine
Orange twist

Combine all ingredients in a mixing glass, add ice, shake and strain into a chilled cocktail glass. Garnish with an orange twist.

THE B&E

A little Dutch courage for a big adventure

1 oz. Sloe gin
1 oz. gin
¾ oz. lemon juice
1 oz. simple syrup
3 to 4 oz. soda water

Mix first four ingredients and pour into ice filled highball glass. Add soda.
Garnish with an orange slice and a cherry.